**The** [barcode: D0292966]

Destined to ru...

Welcome to San Vantino...home to siblings Prince Rini, Prince Vincenzo and Princess Bella Baldasseri. The family may appear to live a charmed life—they're royalty, after all!—but that doesn't mean that every day is smooth sailing.

Now they must face their greatest challenge. Can they devote themselves to their kingdom *and* let themselves find true love? Well...we're about to find out!

Step inside the palace with...

Rini and Luna's story
*Reclaiming the Prince's Heart*
Available now!

Vincenzo and Francesca's story
Bella and Luca's story
Coming soon!

Dear Reader,

Amnesia is a condition that most of us will never experience. I love the book *Random Harvest* by James Hilton. It deals with a man who loses his memory. I don't want to ruin the story by telling you what happened, but it lived with me for years. This last year I decided I would write an amnesia story, though I know nothing about it. My research didn't help me know what it was like, only that it gave me the true story of a man from Ontario, Canada, who experienced it. I've never known anyone who had it, and I couldn't find anyone who had it, so I couldn't interview them. Therefore, this latest book of mine, *Reclaiming the Prince's Heart*, is my version of what could happen.

Enjoy!

*Rebecca Winters*

# *Reclaiming the Prince's Heart*

—

## *Rebecca Winters*

**HARLEQUIN**

*Romance*

# (H) HARLEQUIN®

*Romance*™

Recycling programs for this product may not exist in your area.

ISBN-13: 978-1-335-40680-4

Reclaiming the Prince's Heart

Copyright © 2021 by Rebecca Winters

Harlequin Enterprises ULC
22 Adelaide St. West, 40th Floor
Toronto, Ontario M5H 4E3, Canada
www.Harlequin.com

Printed in U.S.A.

**Rebecca Winters** lives in Salt Lake City, Utah. With canyons and high alpine meadows full of wildflowers, she never runs out of places to explore. They, plus her favorite vacation spots in Europe, often end up as backgrounds for her romance novels—because writing is her passion, along with her family and church. Rebecca loves to hear from readers. If you wish to email her, please visit her website at rebeccawinters.net.

## Books by Rebecca Winters

### Harlequin Romance

#### Secrets of a Billionaire

*The Greek's Secret Heir*
*Unmasking the Secret Prince*

#### Escape to Provence

*Falling for Her French Tycoon*
*Falling for His Unlikely Cinderella*

#### The Princess Brides

*The Princess's New Year Wedding*
*The Prince's Forbidden Bride*
*How to Propose to a Princess*

#### Holiday with a Billionaire

*Captivated by the Brooding Billionaire*
*Falling for the Venetian Billionaire*
*Wedding the Greek Billionaire*

*The Magnate's Holiday Proposal*

Visit the Author Profile page
at Harlequin.com for more titles.

To my dear friend Rachel, whom I believe is an angel on earth, for giving me her undying devotion over the years. Her expertise, her brilliance, her pure heart, her goodness make her exceptional. How blessed are her three children and husband. She listened to my ideas, supported my thoughts and helped with some of the twists and turns of this novel. Everyone loves her as I do.

## Praise for Rebecca Winters

# CHAPTER ONE

*San Vitano, an Italian-speaking country bordering eastern Switzerland and northern Italy. June 2. 6 a.m.*

As RINI EASED himself away from his sleeping, delectable wife, she caught him around the shoulders.

"Not so fast, *mi amore*. Tell me again why you have to go today of all days?"

He kissed her mouth hungrily. "This inspection tour can't be put off any longer. I'm implementing some new safety rules with the chief mining engineer, Gustavo, and his assistants."

"I realize it's important, but this will be the first time we've been apart since our wedding. I already miss you so much, I haven't been able to sleep."

"Why do you think I made love to you

half the night?" he murmured against her lips. He was so in love with Luna, he could stay in bed with her forever. "Just remember, I'll be home at the end of the day."

"You'd better keep your promise. I have something special planned for our six-month wedding anniversary tonight."

He hugged her lovingly. "I wouldn't miss it. As it happens, I have a surprise for you, too. Now, go back to sleep."

After kissing her breathless, he slid out of bed to shower. Once ready in jeans, a work shirt and boots, he walked out the back of the *palazzo* to his waiting helicopter.

The half-hour trip to the King Midas gold-mining site on the Italian, Austrian and Slovenian border didn't take long. The men were there to greet him in the front office. Together they went down into the mine to get busy. By three in the afternoon, Rini's work was done and the men left.

Alone with Gustavo, they walked through the inclined shaft while they talked. "Is there anything else you want to discuss with me, Your Highness?"

"Gustavo, how many times have we had

this conversation in the past? I'm the Crown Prince, not the King. Call me Rini."

He shook his head. "It's impossible to forget. Your new safety rules are going to make a big difference around here."

"I'm glad you approve, and I'm impressed over the excellent job you're doing. Keep me posted on your progress. Now I've got to fly back to Asteria. My wife and I are celebrating our anniversary tonight."

The head mining engineer flashed him a knowing smile. "I don't blame you for being eager. You're still in the honeymoon stage. May it last forever."

Rini chuckled. "Agreed." He couldn't wait to get back home.

They left the winze, which was a connecting shaft at the lower level, and headed for the mine portal above. Suddenly, Rini heard an earsplitting crack that sounded like a runaway train. The earth shook under their feet. It must have gone on for a minute or more. He felt dizzy.

"Earthquake."

"It won't last," Rini muttered. They'd both felt them in this region over the years. The tremors continued. "Let's keep moving until we reach the surface." But the words had barely left his lips when there was another explosive sound like a bomb had gone off and they were both knocked to the ground with force.

Gustavo let out a groan. "This isn't any normal quake, Your Highness."

"You're right. Just keep crawling toward the next shaft. I'm right behind you."

"The ground keeps shifting—I'm terrified!"

"Hang on!" Rini tried to reach him when a wall of rocks came crashing down. Claustrophobic dust filled the interior. Rini could hardly breathe. All had gone completely dark. "Gustavo?" He called to him again. "Gustavo?"

There was no answer. The ground kept shaking and there were boulder-like rocks in front of him, impeding any progress. He kept crying out Gustavo's name. Rini's heart sank to realize the manager had to be partially buried beneath the debris.

"I hope you can hear me, Gustavo. I'm going for help and will be back."

Rini, a top mining engineer graduate from the school of mines in Colorado in the

US, knew the layout of this mine like the back of his hand. It was one of the financial backbones of the Baldasseri royal family of San Vitano dating back three centuries. Rini was in charge.

He knew of another shaft leading out of the winze to an intersecting shaft. From there he could keep going until the opening of the shaft came out on the side of the mountain. Once free, he could get help. It was imperative in order to save Gustavo. Heaven knew how many other miners might have been buried in the horrendous quake.

The tremors continued, creating the rolling swell of the ground. More rocks fell. He kept going on his stomach as he clawed his way up through a winding labyrinth that led to another shaft. A little more progress and the unused shaft would lead to an opening he could see in his mind.

"You've got to keep going," Rini muttered to himself. Gustavo's life depended on it.

Another few feet and large portions of rock started falling on him. One hit his head, sending excruciating pain through his body. "Luna—" he cried her name in desperation before he knew nothing more.

* * *

Luna set the dining room table. Rini would be home from the mine soon. She couldn't wait and wanted everything to be just right. After gift wrapping the positive result of her home pregnancy test, she put it at his place. They'd wanted to start a family. Today she'd found out the joyous news. Luna hadn't had time to see her OB, but she'd call him tomorrow. Tonight she and her husband would celebrate!

Delicious smells of a pork roast filled the *palazzo*. She hurried into the kitchen to check on the potatoes in a half shell. Rini would be eating a meal he'd never had before that included roasted asparagus and stuffed apples. Luna had been born and raised in Scuol, Switzerland. She'd prepared some of her late grandmother's recipes. It would be exciting to serve him something she loved in honor of their becoming parents.

While she arranged the apples in a deep dish, their housekeeper, Viola, came into the kitchen. Her normal ruddy complexion had lost color. "Luna—you'd better come in the salon. The King and Queen are here."

Rini's grandparents had come to the *pala-*

*zzo*? They'd only made an appearance once
before at her and Rini's dinner invitation.
What on earth would have caused them to
do something this unprecedented with no
advanced warning?

She rushed through the *palazzo* to the
salon and found them both seated on the
couch. What could have brought them here?
Luna sat down in a chair opposite them. "I
know you're here because something is se-
riously wrong. Tell me."

The look of devastation on their faces
caused Luna's heart to plunge to her feet.
Leonardo leaned forward. "There was an
earthquake. It affected the mine."

Luna started to feel sick. "Were some of
the miners injured?"

"I'm afraid eight were killed."

Killed? Aghast, she cried, "Did Rini tell
you that?"

He shook his head as Antonia gripped her
husband's arm. "It pains us to the core to tell
you this, but…he was killed, too."

Rini was dead?

*"No—"* Luna jumped to her feet. "That
isn't possible! I don't believe it."

Antonia got up and walked over to put her arm around her. "We don't want to believe it either, but we've had positive confirmation and came over here immediately to tell you."

She turned to her desolate grandmother-in-law. "This couldn't be. Not Rini—" Tears gushed down her cheeks. "He's the love of my life. There's no purpose without him. I can't live without him. Surely, there's been a mistake."

At this point Leonardo walked over and put his arms around both of them. "We know how you feel, darling."

She stared at them both through a blur. "You really believe he was killed?"

"He went down in the mine with the other seven. None of them ever came up again."

"No—no— This is a nightmare. Please tell me this is a nightmare and I'm going to wake up." Her tears had become a river.

"Come and sit down," he murmured, but she couldn't move. She felt numb. The room started to spin.

"Call our doctor and tell him to come here at once," she heard Antonia tell her husband. But the ringing in Luna's ears had grown so loud, everything went black.

In another few minutes she had cognizance of her surroundings again and found herself lying on the couch. There were voices in the room and the palace doctor, Dr. Norelli, came over to her.

"I'm so sorry, Principessa. Stay still while I examine you." He took her vital signs. "You seem to be all right, but you've just undergone a severe shock. You need rest. I'm going to give you a sedative to help you get through the next few days." He left a bottle of pills on the coffee table.

She struggled to sit up. "Doctor—I'm pregnant even though I haven't seen my OB yet." She heard gasps of surprise come from Rini's grandparents. "I don't want to take anything that would hurt my baby."

"Don't worry. What I've got there will do no harm to you or your child."

By now Viola and her husband, Mateo, had come into the salon. The doctor motioned to him. "Come and help me take her upstairs to the bedroom."

Luna slowly got to her feet. "I'm okay and can make it on my own."

"I'm going to stay the night with you," Antonia murmured.

"We'll both stay," the King added.

"No, Leo," his wife implored. "You go back to the palace in case there's more news. I'll stay in touch with you."

Tears fell down his cheeks. "You're sure?"

"Yes."

"Our hearts are with you." The King pressed a kiss to Luna's cheek and left the room with the doctor.

Antonia reached for the pills and looped her arm through Luna's. They walked slowly to the staircase in the foyer.

Luna buried her face against the older woman's shoulder. "Thank you for staying with me tonight. If it weren't for Rini's baby I'm carrying, I'd want to die."

"But for my great-grandchild you're carrying, *I'd* want to die, too."

They reached the master suite and Antonia helped Luna get ready for bed. After swallowing two pills, she climbed under the covers and rested her head against the pillows. Antonia sat on the side of the bed and held her hand.

"There are no words, are there?"

"No," Luna whispered, "but your presence means the world to me. I loved Rini the first moment I met him. It was like magic. He's the great love of my life. To think he died in a mine collapse. How terrifying those moments must have been for him! Oh, Tonia... I can't bear that I've lost him."

Luna broke down in heaving sobs. Loving arms reached over to hug her. They stayed that way for a long time. Eventually, she said, "I'll go to the guest room down the hall and we'll talk in the morning. If you need me during the night, call me on my phone. Now, let the sedative help you sleep." She kissed her forehead and left the bedroom.

The next morning Luna awakened in so much pain, she didn't know why she was alive. She turned to reach for her husband, then realized he wouldn't be coming home and was hit with another unbearable wave of grief.

"Luna?"

Antonia had come into the room with a tray. "I've brought us some coffee and rolls. You need to eat something since you didn't eat dinner last night."

She sat up with tears dripping off her face. "I couldn't. Is there any more news?"

"Leo said search parties worked all night,

hoping to bring out the bodies, but they couldn't penetrate the blockage. There's no way to recover them."

Luna slid her legs over the side of the bed. "I'm a terrible person, Antonia. I've been thinking of myself without giving thought to you or the families of the miners." She looked up at her. "If Rini were alive, he'd be the first one to visit them and try to bring some comfort. As his wife, that's what I need to do."

"That would be a wonderful tribute to them, but not today. You need to take it easy."

"I can't just lie here, Antonia. I'll get dressed and go back to the palace with you. With Leonardo's help, I can gather the names and addresses of the families involved and make plans to visit them during the week. Rini would want this."

"He'd be so proud of you for thinking of them. But I insist you eat and drink a little to keep up your strength."

"I will, but I'm ashamed that I haven't thought of you and Leo or your needs. I should be waiting on you. Rini's your darling grandson. After losing your two sons and another grandson, I don't know how you're handling this. You're the strongest people I've ever known."

She hurried over to the Queen, who had sat down next to a table with the tray. Luna threw her arms around her and they both wept again.

"With lots of love and faith, we got through. You will, too."

"I want to do everything I can so Rini will be proud of me."

"He adored you. After he met you, he told me his life was complete."

"He said that?" she cried through the tears. "Oh—I can't believe he's gone. I just can't believe it, but I have to."

They both drank coffee and bit into Viola's wonderful rolls. "I'll hurry to shower and get ready. Leonardo needs us."

Antonia nodded with fresh tears in her eyes.

"He has already called Rini's cousin Vincenzo with the news."

Luna could understand that. "Vincenzo and Rini are best friends."

"Yes. Leo says he's devastated. With Rini

gone, Vincenzo is the next in line to be the Crown Prince."

Gone… Her beloved husband was gone. The earthquake had changed all their lives.

Luna hurried to the bathroom in agony. She took two more pills, then got into the shower where she broke down sobbing and didn't come out again for a long time.

*June 12*

Luna had been restless since the call from Rini's secretary at the palace. The acting manager of the mine had phoned to convey a message to Luna. A reminder, really. It seemed that one of the lost miners, Jaka Ravenikar, a Slovenian, had been working for the mine on a visa. His family lived near the mine in the border town of Rezana, Slovenia. It was the only family she hadn't visited throughout the past ten days with flowers and the assurance of financial aid to ease their burden.

Luna wanted to travel to Rezana and pay her respects on the monarchy's behalf. This morning she planned to go to the palace and ask Leonardo for help in visiting this family.

She would need assistance, however, since she didn't speak Slovene.

Once that was done, a memorial service for family could be planned for Rini at the palace. But she couldn't accept the fact that she'd lost the love of her life. She never would. A memorial service would mean he was really gone, increasing her pain.

Her own parents had died when she was five in a plane accident. She'd been raised by her wonderful grandparents in Scuol, Switzerland. Her grandfather died first, then her grandmother. The losses had devastated her, but in time she won a scholarship to study business administration at St. Gallen University in Switzerland.

Upon graduation she'd obtained interviews with half a dozen companies. One led her to the Baldasseri Gold Mining Company in Asteria, San Vitano, an Italian-speaking country, where she was offered a position. Luna was bilingual in Italian and Romansh, her native language. Eighty thousand people in the Engadin of Switzerland spoke it. She felt that working there would be a good fit and she liked the staff.

Two weeks after she'd been hired, she met

Prince Rinieri, who was the head gold-mining engineer for the mine. He was also the grandson of the King and Queen of San Vitano and was next in line for the throne. It only took meeting him to fall madly in love. They soon married and life couldn't have been more beautiful until tragedy struck. She could still see the article in the newspaper.

*Crown Prince Rinieri Francesco Baldasseri of San Vitano was killed during an 8.7 earthquake at the King Midas Mine near the Slovenian border.*

*He leaves behind his loving wife of six months, Her Royal Highness, Princess Luna Biancho Baldasseri.*

*World leaders send their condolences to her and Their Royal Highnesses King Leonardo and Queen Antonia Baldasseri.*

For the past week she'd hoped and prayed that by some miracle the bodies would at least be found, but they'd been buried too deeply. As for Luna, in her mind and heart *he was still missing.* A part of her refused to believe he was dead. Maybe it was because of a dream she'd had where Rini appeared to her. It had seemed so real, she couldn't shake it.

Still racked with debilitating grief that attacked her in waves, she stepped into the shower to get ready, then styled her white-blond hair. She wore it neck length from a center part. Before the quake, she'd let it hang down her back the way Rini loved it. But a few days ago, in a surge of pain and disbelief that he was gone, she'd taken the scissors and had started cutting.

When she looked in the mirror, she saw a pale ghost of the woman she'd once been. She'd lost weight due to her anguish and her morning sickness. Her OB had warned her she needed to eat now that she was pregnant. He'd given her medication to help. Luna knew she had to live for herself and for Rini's baby.

Without wasting another moment, she reached for her phone on the bedside table and called the Queen to alert her she was coming. The older woman's love and support had made it possible for Luna to survive these past ten days of sheer agony.

"Luna?"

"*Buongiorno*, Tonia." They'd been on a first-name basis since Rini had introduced his grandmother to her eight months ago. "Forgive me for disturbing you, but this can't wait."

"What is it?"

"I have a favor to ask of Leonardo." She explained what it was she wanted to do to honor the miner. "I didn't know one of the men was a Slovenian. I hadn't realized he'd been working there on a work visa."

"I didn't either, Luna. Of course, Leo will arrange it. Come as soon as you can and we'll both talk to him."

"Thank you so much. Since we've met all the families of the other miners from San Vitano, I'd like to fly there and meet his family, take them flowers."

"I don't see a problem."

Relief filled Luna. "Wonderful. I'll be over within a half hour."

Once she'd hung up, she phoned for her driver to meet her in front of the *palazzo*. Then she rushed to the closet to dress in an aqua-colored, short-sleeved, two-piece summer suit. She matched it with white sandals and grabbed her purse.

"Viola?" she called to the housekeeper when she hurried downstairs to the foyer. "I'm leaving for the palace. I'm not sure when I'll be back, but I'll let you know."

Before long she reached the palace and met Antonia outside Leonardo's private study. The two walked in on him. "Leo?"

He lifted his gray head. Despair was written all over him. "Cara? Luna?"

"Luna has come to ask for a favor."

"Of course. Anything." He held out his arms and Luna ran into them. "How are you doing, darling?"

She wiped her eyes. "The same as you."

"Then that means you're in pain. None of us was ready for losing him."

"No. I never will be. Rini's been the light of my life and yours." Luna sat down on the love seat next to Antonia. "His secretary let me know that one of the miners was Slovenian."

He nodded. "That's right."

"I want to fly there today if possible and pay our respects to the man's family."

"Bless you for thinking of it."

"There's just one thing, Leonardo," Luna added. "I would need a translator to go with me since I don't speak Slovene."

"You know Carlo. He's my official foreign emissary and fluent in half a dozen languages. I'll send him with you."

"That would be wonderful!" Luna cried. "He's one of Rini's favorites, and mine."

Leonardo nodded. "I'll ask him to arrange your flight to Rezana and pick up the flowers. He can arrange a car and escorts to meet you when you arrive there."

"Oh, thank you. The secretary gave me the address and phone number of Jaka's family."

"Plan to leave from here in two hours."

"You're wonderful." Luna flew off the love seat and ran to throw her arms around him once more. "I love you."

"We love you, too. You and the baby are all we have left of our Rini."

Luna walked out with Antonia, who pulled her aside. "Thank you for remembering this. It makes Leo happy to do something positive."

"I feel the same way. Right now I'll go home to gather a few things, then I'll be back and meet you out at the helipad behind the palace." She hugged her grandmother-in-law again before rushing out of the palace.

Two hours later Luna had been strapped into the royal helicopter with Carlo Bruni. The man had served in the San Vitano Military besides having all the leadership qualities Rini had admired. Luna had always liked him and felt comfortable with him as they flew to Rezana, the town two miles away from the mine.

Rini had called it the Re Mida Mine, named for King Midas. Luna had worked for the mining company business office in Asteria, San Vitano's capital city, but she'd never traveled to the actual mine. Rini had once told her the mountainous terrain there was full of a network of caves. Most of the system was located next to the Slovenian border, with dozens of little settlements clustered on top of the northern rim like a medieval town. Rezana was one of them.

She looked out the window during the descent. Her heart lurched to realize her beloved husband had been caught in the earthquake and lay deep in the rubble that had robbed him and the others of life. Fighting not to break down, she bit her knuckle while they landed.

A driver and government official met them at the small airport, engaging Carlo in conversation. He eventually turned to her. "Since I'm Leonardo's emissary, their government is giving us assistance by escorting us to the Ravenikar home."

"That's very kind of them."

He opened the car door and they got in. The other car followed. Soon, they wound around to a home in the small, picturesque town. They were met out in front by Jaka's father.

"This is Anton Ravenikar," Carlo translated for Luna.

The father of the dead miner looked at the two of them through eyes filled with tears. Luna walked up to him. "My name is Luna Baldasseri. I'm the wife of Rinieri Baldasseri, who was inspecting the mine when the quake struck. I know you're suffering, Mr. Ravenikar. So am I."

He nodded.

Unable to hold back she asked, "When your country searched for Jaka's body, did they see any other bodies?"

She waited while Carlo translated. Turning to her he said, "No, but he wouldn't know because he couldn't help in the search."

Luna closed her eyes for a second. "Ask him if there's someone who *would* know."

Carlo translated again. Anton muttered something.

"What did he say?"

"We should ask Zigo, a policeman at the station. He was Jaka's friend and helped in the search. He could tell you definitively how it went."

It had been a long shot. Of course there was no news. "Thank you so much. Please know how sorry we are for your loss."

He nodded. "Thank you for coming. It means everything."

Carlo translated the man's appreciation that she'd come. Anton invited them inside the house. She learned that Jaka had been married and living with his parents and an older brother and sister. When Luna presented the flowers to Jaka's widow, everyone burst into tears. The family couldn't have been more grateful and thrilled for the visit and the promise of a financial donation.

Once it ended, they went outside to the

car. Carlo murmured, "If you wish, we'll go to police headquarters where you can talk to Zigo before we go home. Do you want to do that?"

"I'm sure he won't be able to tell us anything, but I admit I'd still like to talk to him for a minute." The need to learn anything more was the driving factor for her. *And the dream that had seemed so real*.

"Then let's go."

# CHAPTER TWO

ONCE INSIDE THE BUILDING, Luna and Carlo were shown to the front office of the station. She looked around and smiled at two officers. Carlo asked if they could speak to Zigo.

The younger one came forward. Luna's heart raced as they were all introduced. "Zigo? Do you speak Italian?"

*"Cosi-cosi."*

His answer, "so-so," was better than nothing. She stared into his eyes. *"Did you* look for Jaka Ravenikar?"

*"Sì.* He was friend."

Her pulse picked up speed. "Did you see any bodies?"

"No bodies," he answered without hesitation.

A little moan escaped her lips. "I'm looking for my *marito.*"

At this point Carlo had to translate.

Zigo said, "He died, too?"

Her eyes filled with tears. "My husband didn't come home. Maybe he escaped." Was it possible?

He frowned. "Escaped?"

"Got away." She used her fingers to show him that her husband might have gotten out. Again, Carlo translated.

"Ah," he said. "No. I know nothing."

With her hopes dashed, she asked if she could use the restroom before they got back on the helicopter. Carlo interceded. Zigo nodded and showed Luna where to go.

They walked down a hallway to the rear of the station. She went in to freshen up and say a little prayer to help her get through the rest of this day.

When Luna came out of the restroom, she found Zigo waiting for her near the end of the hall. "*Grazie* for talking to me."

He nodded.

Filled with fresh pain, Luna hurried into the front office. Together she and Carlo left for the car to drive them to the helicopter. As she started to get into the backseat, she heard the cry, "Principessa?" She turned to see who was calling out. To her surprise it was Zigo. He'd run after them.

"Carlo?" she said. "Zigo's Italian is sketchy. Speak to him in Slovene and find out what he's trying to tell me."

A long conversation ensued. She couldn't imagine.

"Luna—when you told the guard you hoped Rini had escaped, it made him think."

She blinked. "What are you saying?"

"A day after the earthquake there was talk of a stranger who was brought into the town by a motorist on the highway. He'd discovered a man wounded and lying at the side of the highway. Our station was called. We responded and took him to the local hospital. So far no one has identified him."

Her heart leaped. "Is he still there?"

More talk ensued. Carlo turned to her. "As far as Zigo knows, he hasn't left, but the man spoke a strange language neither he nor the officer understood."

A strange language? That didn't sound like Rini. Still, this could be something of vital interest for all of them. Maybe it was one of the miners from San Vitano who'd managed to get out. Maybe one of them knew a different language.

"Zigo says they are looking for anyone who might know him. The man had no papers on him, no way to identify him. When you told Zigo you were looking for your husband and hoped he'd escaped the cave-in, it got him thinking, and—"

"And he thinks it might be Rini!" she cried out for joy, interrupting him.

"Zigo didn't say that, especially when the man didn't respond to any languages other officers had tried with him. But he felt your distress. Don't get your hopes up, Luna."

"I can't help it."

"I know," he said in a kind voice.

Luna couldn't imagine the stranger being her Rini. She bit her lip. "I'm thinking it's one of the miners from our country. I can't even imagine how wonderful it would be to find one of them alive. Ask Zigo if we can see him."

After the inquiry, the answer came back that they could proceed directly to the hospital. She and Carlo got back into the car while Zigo gave instructions to the driver, and said he'd alert the staff. He eyed Luna with compassion before waving them off. A few minutes later they arrived at the hospital.

Thankful for the cooperation, they hurried inside and were met by a woman who showed them to the second floor. They were taken inside an office and told to wait.

After she left, Luna grasped Carlo's arm. "What if it's one of the miners? He could tell us what happened in the mine. He'll be able to tell us about Rini." Her eyes filled with tears. "I'd give anything for the tiniest bit of information about their last moments."

"Let's pray for that much good news, Luna. But remember they said he didn't speak a language they understood."

"I know."

Before long, a man of probably sixty joined them. He spoke to Carlo at some length. Finally, he turned to Luna and spoke to her in Italian.

"It's an honor to meet you, Principessa Baldasseri. I'm Doctor Miakar. I understand your husband has been missing since the earthquake. If this man is the Crown Prince of San Vitano, the government will be anxious to learn what you tell us and cooperate with you any way they can."

"Thank you so much."

"Right now he's under sedation and sleeping. I had to operate on his arm, which is badly infected. He was so agitated, I was forced to give him something to calm him down. He should be awake within ten or fifteen minutes. Come with me so you can see if you recognize him."

With her heart thundering, she and Carlo followed him down the hall to an examination room. He opened the door.

Her eyes flew to the black-haired man in his late twenties lying asleep on the gurney, dressed in hospital greens and socks. His head was turned away. An IV had been hooked up to fight the infection in his arm.

She walked around the bed to see him clearly, then almost fainted.

*"Rini—"*

Carlo grabbed Luna's arm to support her. In a shaken voice he said, "It *is* His Royal Highness. You were inspired to come to Rezana, Luna."

"My beloved Rini." She couldn't believe it. *He was alive! Rini had come to her in her dream!* Joy radiated through her. "He didn't die. God has heard my prayers."

She'd never seen him with ten days' growth of beard and disheveled hair. Nothing could hide the pallor of his gaunt complexion. He'd suffered weight loss. Her gorgeous six-foot-three husband normally weighed two hundred and ten pounds. But none of it mattered because she'd found him and would take perfect care of him until he was well and restored to his former dashing self.

As she leaned over with the intent to kiss him, the doctor cautioned her not to touch him. "He needs the sleep. That will give us time to talk. Come back to my office."

It killed her to leave him when she'd just found him, but she did as the doctor asked. Her heart was thudding too hard to be healthy. The three of them walked back to the doctor's office.

"So your husband *is* the Crown Prince of San Vitano."

"Yes!" she cried, overjoyed to the point the tears were gushing. "Here." She pulled the wallet out of her purse and handed pictures of him to the doctor to prove it.

He studied them and nodded. "I'll inform the staff and the police. They'll inform the prime minister. Now that we know his identity, he'll be released to you. But we must talk fast, Princess Baldasseri. I need your input."

"Of course. Go on."

"Besides the deep gash on his arm, my examination has revealed he suffered a blow to the back of the head. He also lost a great deal of blood and is still recovering. But I am only a general doctor. This village hospital doesn't have the sophisticated equipment to diagnose him. When you get him home, he needs all kinds of care and must see a neurological specialist right away. You will need a medevac helicopter to transport him back to San Vitano."

"I understand and am so thankful you've been here to take care of him. There are no words to tell you how grateful I am." She turned to Carlo. "I'll call the King and Queen to let them know he's alive. Leonardo will send a medical helicopter immediately."

She pulled out her cell and phoned Rini's grandparents, who were speechless with joy when they heard the news. They all wept for a long time.

"I'll explain everything later. Right now

Carlo is here with me and we're at the hospital with the doctor treating Rini, who has a deep cut on his arm. It's infected and they're giving him an antibiotic." She heard Antonia cry out in pain. "Can you send a neurosurgeon with the helicopter? We also need to know how soon to expect it."

"It will arrive there within the hour," Leonardo promised. "A miracle happened today, and all because of you. You have no idea the measure of our gratitude for you."

"I love you both. We have our Rini back. It's a glorious day."

"Indeed it is. Come home safely, my dear. We'll have everything ready for you at the hospital."

She hung up and related the news to the doctor. "Can I sit with my husband until he's transferred?"

"I don't see why not but realize he's very nervous and trusts no one. We can't communicate with him. When you get home, he'll need medical help to see to his immediate needs."

"Thank you for taking such wonderful care of him, Doctor Miakar. We'll make sure you and the hospital are recompensed for all you've done."

"It's an honor."

"We're going to be here for a while," Carlo murmured to her. "I'll have the driver take me to the helicopter and tell them to fly home. Then I'll return for you and we'll wait for the other helicopter. It will land here at the hospital."

"You're a treasure, Carlo. I couldn't have done this without you."

After he left the hospital, she turned to the doctor. "Can I see my husband now?"

He indicated she should follow him. Luna was living to see Rini again and just fill her eyes. The wonder of his being alive consumed her.

When she went back to his room and sat down by him, she realized he hadn't moved. It gave her the opportunity to feast her hungry eyes on his face and body. The first time she'd met him, she knew the tall, hunky, black-haired Crown Prince had to be the most attractive man alive.

"Rini—" she sobbed his name quietly, unable to imagine how horrible his life must have been since the earthquake. Why couldn't he speak or understand anything? They said he spoke a strange language. She couldn't get over it.

Luna walked around to see the top of his head. The doctor said he'd received a blow. She couldn't detect anything with all that black hair covering his scalp. Who knew what horrors he'd had to live through?

He was hooked up to an IV, and one of the nursing staff was checking his vital signs. After a while Luna could tell he was coming to because he moved his strong legs and turned his head to the other side of the pillow.

She moved to the other side of his bed to be close to him. Without thinking, she whispered, *"Jeu carezel tei, Rini,"* in her native language. It meant *I love you*.

Suddenly, he opened those translucent gray eyes she'd thought she'd never see again. They stared at her without recognition. She assumed it was because he was still sedated. *"Ti discurras rumantch?"*

Her heart turned over because he'd heard her outpouring of love and understood. He'd just asked her if she spoke Romansh. *That* was the strange language no one understood?

"*Gea*. Yes, yes, yes."

"How come no one else can communicate? Where am I? I've been going insane that no one understands me. But *you* do. Why? Do you know me?"

His questions were fired one after another. The last question shocked her, but now was not the time to try and understand what was going on.

"I know you very well." Her voice shook. "Your name is Rini and I'm your wife, Luna."

An incredulous expression entered his intelligent eyes. "Impossible! I've never been married."

Help. Something was terribly wrong. *Don't panic, Luna.* "Thank heaven you're alive and that I've found you. You're in a hospital in Rezana, Slovenia. I'm going to take you home. A helicopter is on the way."

At that moment Carlo appeared at the door. He motioned her to come out into the hall. Her gaze shot back to her precious husband, who was so disoriented, she realized he was still under the effects of the anesthetic. "I have to leave you for a few minutes."

"You *can't* go. No one else understands

me." He sounded utterly frantic. It wrenched her heart.

"I promise I'll see you in a few minutes. Trust me."

Trust her?

That breathtaking blonde woman, a stranger, had just said she was his wife? How could that possibly be? No man could forget her if he'd been married to her. He realized he must be dreaming. It had to be the anesthetic that had put him to sleep and he'd started to hallucinate.

What was he doing in Slovenia? No words had made sense to him until he heard a voice say that she loved him. Those were the first words he'd understood since waking up in the hospital. Whoever she really was, he would have to trust her all right since she was his lifeline to get out of here.

A nurse came in to check his vital signs again. He kept waiting for the woman named Luna to return. To finally be able to talk to someone, and then she had to leave the room. He'd go out of his mind waiting for her to come back.

What if she didn't?

He broke out in a cold sweat.

The nurse looked worried as she checked his blood pressure. After she'd listened to his heart, she left the room. *Damn.* How long did he have to remain in this limbo?

When he was about ready to pull out the IV and leave the room on his own to find this Luna, a strange man came in wearing a business suit. "Rini?"

According to Luna, Rini was his name.

The man smiled and patted his own chest. "I'm Doctor Romano."

Romano? It meant nothing to him.

The man came around to check Rini's skull. His hands were gentle, but Rini's crown had been tender since he'd awakened in the hospital. The slight probing hurt. What was going on?

He nodded to Rini before leaving the room. Now what? Another endless wait?

Before long two male hospital workers came inside. They removed the IV and wheeled him out of the room and down the hall to an elevator. Once on the main floor, he was taken down another hall and outside where he saw a medevac helicopter standing by.

Where in the hell was Luna? Where was he being taken? He tried to get off the gurney, but they restrained him.

Luna and Carlo stayed in Dr. Miakar's office, waiting to hear what would happen next. Soon, another man came inside. He smiled at Luna.

"Principessa Baldasseri?" He spoke Italian. "I'm Doctor Piero Romano from the Sacred Heart Hospital in San Vitano."

"Oh, thank goodness you're here!" She took in the fiftyish-looking brown-haired man standing there in a business suit. "You must be the neurosurgeon my grandfather-in-law sent. It was marvelous of you to come at a moment's notice when I know how busy you must be. Thank you more than you know."

"I'm honored to have been asked to help your husband. I just wanted to say that San Vitano was devastated over the reported death of the Crown Prince. I don't have to tell you how overjoyed the King and Queen are to learn that he's alive and will be returning. The country will celebrate the moment it hears their favorite son is alive. But I dare say no one is happier than you."

"You're right. No one could know how I'm feeling at this moment." Tears gushed down her cheeks.

"I've already checked your husband."

"You've seen him?"

"I have, and we're going to take good care of him. Before we leave in the helicopter, however, there are things I need to tell you. I spoke briefly with Doctor Miakar and we looked at your husband's record of confinement. I'll know a lot more when I get him scanned, but one thing is clear. He's suffering from amnesia."

"Amnesia…" She stared at him in alarm, unable to comprehend it. *That* was the reason he didn't understand anything?

"I need information. What languages does he speak, Principessa?"

She brushed the moisture off her cheeks. "Please call me Luna."

"If you wish."

"I do. My husband speaks Italian, German, Slovene, English and Romansh."

"Romansh?"

"Yes. It's my native language and Rini

learned it living at his second cousin's home in Switzerland. When I first saw him a little while ago, I told him I loved him in Romansh. He opened his eyes, shocked that I spoke a language he could understand."

"Wonderful. You're going to be the great key to helping him."

"But shouldn't he have recovered his memory since the quake? Surely, it ought to be returning by now."

"Not necessarily."

Paralyzing pain swept through her. Now that he'd explained everything, Luna was starting to understand why Rini had fired all those questions at her. It was incomprehensible to her. All of it.

"Doctor Romano, you don't mean he might never regain it—" she half groaned the words "—that he'll never recognize me or his world?"

"We don't know. I've read of a case history of a man living in Canada who had a blow to the head and forgot who he was. It's called a fugue state, and very rare. Years later he suddenly remembered who he was, but he'd been missing for years."

Years…

"Perhaps when your husband is transferred to familiar surroundings, he'll remember everything. But if he doesn't, then you need to be aware of his condition and prepare yourself that recognition might not happen right away. For now, we'll take it a step at a time."

Another moan escaped her lips. Rini might never recognize her? How could that be? She shuddered.

"As soon as we arrive at the hospital, he'll be taken to the suite reserved for the King where everything will be done for him. The history on him says he's manageable if you give him time to think about it."

"What do you mean by that?"

"He's lost his memory and doesn't know what's happened to him. It has made him paranoid because he hasn't been able to communicate with anyone until now. Doctor Miakar described that condition exactly. Your husband is a tall, strong man, so it's doubly important we try to keep him as calm as possible until we've worked with him. It's no wonder he's skittish."

Rini skittish? That didn't sound like the husband she knew. Out of all the things that could have happened to him, having amnesia would never have been a possibility in her mind. She turned to the doctor. "He must be terrified not to remember anything! I can't imagine it."

He eyed her with compassion. "Exactly."

Her body trembled. "I'm frightened, Doctor Romano."

"Of course you are, but I'm here to help you as well as your husband. With the aid of Doctor Tullia, an outstanding neuropsychologist I've asked to be on this case, you'll be able to deal with a situation new to all of you. If you're ready, we'll go out to the helicopter."

The medevac helicopter team helped the three of them climb in and strapped them in along the side. Her heart pounded hard as Rini was brought out to the helicopter and lifted to the airbed.

"Luna!" he cried when he saw her. "I thought you'd gone."

Oh, Rini, Rini. "I promised I wouldn't leave you," she said in Romansh.

"Where have you been?" His eyes probed hers.

"Talking to the doctors. But you're going

home now. Try to relax. It's only a half-hour flight."

Her husband was returning wrapped in hospital green Slovenian swaddling clothes. Where were his own clothes, let alone his wedding ring and watch?

After the helicopter lifted off, Rini held her gaze. "How did we meet?"

"It's a long story. I was born in Scuol, Switzerland, where we speak Italian and Romansh. You have a second cousin Vincenzo, who also lives in Scuol and you learned to speak it.

"I started working for your company. You and I spoke Romansh on the first day we met. When you found out I'd been born in Scuol, it gave us a unique connection. We often spoke it so no one else could understand." It was their private language of love. In truth, it had been love at first sight for them, but he didn't want to hear that now.

"I don't have any family."

Oh, dear. Too much information. "Don't worry about that right now."

Before long they reached the Sacred Heart Hospital in Asteria and landed on the roof, where attendants were waiting.

"We're here, Rini."

"Where?"

"At the hospital in your hometown. You need to be taken care of for a little while longer."

His features hardened. "I don't want to be in another hospital."

"Just for a little while until I know you'll be all right. That infection was a bad one."

"Where will you be?"

"Right here with you. But first you must go with Doctor Romano. I'll join you in a minute."

"You swear it?" The demand broke her heart. He was so paranoid it frightened her.

Oh, Rini. Darling. "I swear."

The doctor got out of the helicopter first to accompany Rini, who was wheeled inside to the top-floor suite of the hospital. With security everywhere, she knew the King and Queen had been waiting on the premises.

She and Carlo followed. When they emerged from the elevator, Antonia cried Luna's name and ran to her. They hugged and cried tears together. "Where's Leonardo?"

"Doctor Romano is talking to him while

another doctor is taking care of the gash on Rini's arm and getting him settled. They're already talking over a plan of tests and will call in a nutritionist to get him healthy again. When I glimpsed him, I must admit I hardly recognized my grandson with facial hair and weight loss."

"I know. It's a shock. Before we go in to him, there's something of vital importance you should know first." They hurried toward the door to the suite and walked inside. Dr. Romano saw them and motioned them over to him and the King.

Rini's grandfather wept, but it wasn't for joy. Not this time. Luna turned to Dr. Romano. "Will you tell my grandmother-in-law your diagnosis?"

"Tell me what?" the older woman murmured.

In the next few minutes the doctor explained that Rini had amnesia and how careful they would have to be to hide their alarm. Luna's heart went out to them, but she knew Rini was desperate for her to come to him, and no wonder. He couldn't talk to anyone else! "May I go in to him right now?"

The doctor nodded. "Go ahead. We'll come in soon."

After giving Leonardo a hug, she hurried into the room where Rini lay on the bed. He shot up when he saw her. "Where is this hospital?"

"This is the Sacred Heart Hospital in Asteria, San Vitano."

"San Vitano?"

She moaned. "It's the country on the Italian-Swiss border where you were born and live."

None of it seemed to make an impression. Her beloved husband looked so bewildered she wanted to cry buckets but couldn't. Not in front of him.

"Where's the doctor who operated on my arm?"

"He's at the hospital in Rezana, Slovenia, where you were taken to treat your gash and get antibiotics."

"How long do I have to be in this hospital?"

They were getting into dangerous territory. "If you'll wait a minute, I'll get the doctor, who will answer a lot of your questions."

"Wait—"

"Rini—I promise I'll be right back." She

didn't know how much to tell him. This was uncharted territory.

Nervous, yet excited out of her mind that she had her husband back, she left the room and found the doctor talking with Rini's grandparents. They turned to her and gave her another hug. She knew they were dying to see Rini.

"Doctor Romano? Rini has so many questions. So do I. What I don't understand is, how's it possible that he doesn't remember any of the other languages he knows?"

The doctor shook his head. "I can't explain how amnesia works, but what's happened is miraculous for him and you. Your being able to get through to him speaking Romansh is going to make all the difference in his recovery. It'll mean you need to be around him constantly and serve as his translator."

"I'm his wife and there's nothing I want more." She smiled. "Right now he's so loaded with questions, it worries me. I don't know what I should tell him."

"Understood," the doctor replied. "And it's true we don't want to overload him. I'll go in to talk to him." He turned to Rini's grandparents. "In a few minutes I'll ask the two of you to come in."

Leonardo nodded. "We'll be waiting."

"I won't be long. Now I must see to our patient." His comment relieved Luna. She led the way.

# CHAPTER THREE

RINI WAS STILL sitting up in bed, looking so wonderful despite what had happened to him, she had trouble containing her joy. "I told you I'd be back, Rini. I'll translate for Doctor Romano."

The doctor stood next to him. "I know you have hundreds of questions. I'll try to answer some of them. First of all, you ended up in a hospital in Rezana because ten days ago you were deep inside a mine when an earthquake hit the region near the Italian-Slovenian border. Your head suffered a blow. By some miracle you made it out, but your mind has forgotten a lot of information."

"In other words, I now have amnesia." He spoke with a dry irony that was so reminiscent of her brilliant, super-intelligent husband, she smiled.

The doctor turned to her. "There's nothing wrong with his thought processes." Then he turned back to Rini. "You're twenty-nine years old and answer to the name Rinieri Baldasseri."

"Everyone calls you Rini," Luna interjected.

His penetrating gray orbs played over her. *"Co haveis vus num?"*

She took a deep breath. "Yes, I have a name. It's Luna Biancho Baldasseri." So saying, she pulled out four wallet-size photos of the two of them. After studying them, he handed three of them back and kept the one of them kissing, which he put on the bedside table.

"How old are you?"

"Twenty-six."

"Do we have children?"

"Not yet." She didn't dare say anything about the baby yet. "We were only married six months when you left to inspect the Baldasseri King Midas Gold Mine and got caught in the quake."

"Why was I inspecting a mine?"

"Because you're a gold-mining engineer."

"A what?"

"It's true! You graduated from the Colorado School of Mines in the US and you are the head of the three-hundred-year-old gold mine for your family. It's one of the mainstays of your country. But right now you have grandparents who adore you and are anxiously waiting outside to see you."

He pondered the information. "Where are my parents?"

"They passed away four years ago."

"Do I have siblings?"

"You had a brother, Paolo, who was a year older than you. When you were nine and ten, you both ran out in the road to chase your dog at the beach. A bus came by and accidentally killed him and the dog."

When Rini didn't respond she said, "But you have cousins, including your favorite, Vincenzo, you don't remember. He's a year younger than you and was recently engaged to be married."

She turned to the doctor, afraid maybe she'd said too much. "I told him he has grandparents who'd like to see him. What do you think?"

"Why not ask him how he feels right now? Remember that they'll ask questions. If this is too much, it can wait until tomorrow."

She focused on Rini once more. "Would you rather rest now and see your grandparents another time?"

"No. After staying in that hospital for so long, I can't learn enough fast enough."

That sounded like her dynamic husband. "I'll tell them to come in."

She hurried over to the door and motioned for them to enter. "He knows you're his grandparents, but not *who* you are if you understand my meaning. I'll translate for you."

They walked toward Rini, their eyes brimming with tears. "We thought you had died," Antonia said, breaking down.

Leonardo cleared his throat. "Thank the Almighty you're alive and back home with us where you belong."

Rini studied the two of them. "There were many days I wondered where I came from, let alone tried to imagine where I belonged."

"We want you to get better and will do whatever we can to help you. The doctor wants you to stay in the hospital until all the tests are done and you're feeling well enough to go home."

The love in Leonardo's voice touched Luna to the core.

*"Engraziel,"* he answered in Romansh, meaning *thank you*. She translated for his grandparents.

It was Rini's handsome face behind the hair on his head and face. It was his tall, magnificent yet underweight body inside those ghastly mint-green hospital pants and top. It was his deep, thrilling voice that came out of that compelling mouth... But the man they all loved and adored wasn't there.

Her gaze met Dr. Romano's. He'd done his best to warn her about Rini's paranoia. She turned to her husband, who had to be exhausted. "We'll leave so the staff can get your medical regimen going."

"Stay with me." He almost growled the words with an intensity that bespoke his great need.

She wanted to throw herself into his arms and love him into oblivion. "I promise I'll only say goodbye to them. Then I'll be back."

"Luna?" his grandmother said in an aside once they were out in the hall. "We're going to return to the palace and leave you with Rini. What has happened to him is beyond tragic and it's obvious he needs you to communicate. Leo and I will phone the family to let them know everything that has happened. I know Vincenzo will want to come and help do some translating."

That might be helpful for Rini. He'd have another person to talk to. Maybe it was possible he'd recognize Vincenzo. She prayed that would happen.

"Keep us posted." Antonia gave her another hug.

"You know I will, and we'll have a long talk." She hugged Leonardo before they both left. The doctor walked them to the elevator.

Free to be alone with Rini at last, Luna hurried to his room. She took a deep breath and pulled up a chair near the side of the bed. She'd rather climb under the covers with him, even if he didn't know her. "You must feel like a baby who's just been born. All these strange people looking down at you in your crib."

She'd hoped he would chuckle, but he didn't. Their happy marriage had been filled with laughter, but no longer.

"Since we had to fly a certain distance by helicopter, how did you know I'd been taken to a hospital there?"

"I didn't." She leaned forward. "After the quake, seven of the miners turned up missing. One of them was Slovenian, who worked for your company on a visa. You're the head of the Baldasseri Gold Mining Company near the Slovenian border. You'd gone there to do an inspection and implement new reforms."

"None of that computes to me."

"I know." She fought not to break down. "To my horror you were caught in the cave-in, too, or so we thought. There were search parties to bring out the bodies, but none were found. I wanted to interview the Slovenian family, who might be able to shed some light on their missing son because I refused to give up on you."

"I take it I didn't beat you often. Otherwise you wouldn't have bothered to try and find me."

He said it without a smile, but there was nothing wrong with the sense of humor she'd always loved. Maybe there was hope for a happy marriage in time.

"In another week we were going to have a family memorial service for you, Rini, but I was dreading it. I had to be certain you weren't alive somewhere. One night I had a dream that you came to me. It gave me hope."

Rini groaned. "To be frank, I'd hoped never to wake up after they gave me a shot at the other hospital."

That hurt. Her eyes clouded over. "Are you still sorry?"

"I'm trying to process everything."

She looked down, cut to the quick. "There are a lot of people who love you and are thankful you're alive. Your grandparents adore you and can't wait to have a conversation with you, but they realize it will have to be on your timetable."

He didn't respond. "I met a policeman named Zigo, who took you to the hospital. His kindness brought me to you." Her voice caught when she said, "I came close to fainting when I saw you asleep in that hospital room. You've suffered terribly with a gash like that, and the blow to the crown of your head. Are you in horrible pain?"

"No. I was given painkillers."

"Luna?" another voice sounded. She lifted her head. Dr. Romano had come into the room. "Since your husband seems wide awake, I'd like to talk to him for a minute before his dinner is brought in. Would you ask him if it's all right?"

She nodded and turned to Rini. "Are you up for a visit with Doctor Romano? Afterward, they'll bring you a meal."

"If it will get me out of the hospital sooner, why not?" The edgy brittleness of his tone was to be expected, but this part of Rini was unlike the man she'd married.

"He says yes, Doctor."

The older man pulled up a chair on the other side of the bed. "I'm going to record our conversation for my records." Dr. Romano pulled out a tiny recorder. "I'd like you to think back to your first memory."

Rini could hardly concentrate as he looked at the gorgeous woman seated by his side. She'd appeared in his hospital room in Rezana like a vision. Now she'd planted herself next to him in this hospital in Asteria. Her stunning blond beauty and perfection of female form had taken his breath. When she'd told him she loved him, he'd almost gone into cardiac arrest. Until her presence in the Rezana operating room, he'd come close to giving up on life.

In order to concentrate right now, he closed his eyes.

"I remember being in total darkness, completely disoriented. My head hurt like hell. The silence was terrifying because I realized I was alone and the ground beneath me was shaking. I didn't know what I was doing or what was going on. I thought maybe I was dead and in hell."

Luna put a hand to her mouth to silence her sobs, but she had to translate for both of them.

"What did you do at that point, Rini?"

"I don't know exactly, Doctor. My legs were buried under something. It took what seemed like hours for me to remove what felt like rocky debris. Finally, I could move and made some progress. Then I slept for a long time.

"When I awakened, I realized nothing had changed. It frightened the daylights out of me until I discovered I was breathing fresh air. That had to mean there was some kind of exit out of that hellhole I'd been in."

Dr. Romano cleared his throat. "You now know you'd been in an earthquake inside a mine. After all you've been through, your existence is a miracle."

"It is!" Luna exclaimed. Inside she was dying for him and what he'd lived through.

"Go on if you can. Tell us what happened next."

"I kept crawling until I discovered myself lying on vegetation. I felt thistle-like scratches on my hands. There were more earth tremors. When I looked up, I saw a sky full of stars before I fell asleep again. Obviously, I must have slept all night because sunlight woke me up. I realized I was on a mountain, but I didn't know why or where I was. Nothing looked familiar."

"I can't imagine it." Luna moaned the words.

"Neither could I."

"Continue on if you can," the doctor prodded him.

"The crown and right side of my head had bled like the devil. Blood still dripped down my face. I had cuts all over my hands and arms. My gold watch was broken. I didn't even know I had one or when I'd bought it, let alone where. All I felt was a terrible thirst. When I got up, I could barely walk, but I needed help from someone or to find a stream.

"After a while I came to a highway and followed it until I tripped and fell. The next thing I knew, a car came by and stopped. A man got out to talk to me. He spoke a language I didn't understand. He tried to be kind and helped me into his car. I was in and out of it before being driven to a hospital.

"No one in there could understand me, or me them. I lost track of time over the next few days. I couldn't eat and felt too sick to do anything."

Rini opened his eyes. "That's about it."

The doctor got to his feet. "Thank you for bearing with me. Now it's time for you to freshen up and enjoy your dinner. When you're helped into the shower, try not to get that bandage wet they've put on your arm. Also, be careful of your head when you shampoo your hair so it won't hurt your wound. I'll be back in the morning to order some tests. They will tell me a lot more about your head injury."

After Luna translated, Rini said to her, "*You* can't leave!" His eyes blazed as he stared at her. She saw fear in them and understood she was the only person he could communicate with right now.

"Don't worry. I'll be back soon."

"Tonight?"

"Yes, Rini. Tonight. I promise."

She walked out with the doctor, who told her the agenda for the next day. He'd scheduled a series of scans. "Now that he's home, you can feel comfortable in telling him whatever he wants or needs to know. Don't hold back. We'll see how he gets along."

When they parted, Luna phoned for her driver and went home to the *palazzo* to pack some items for Rini.

That look of fear had her rushing to the hospital once more. He was the most confident, in-charge man she'd ever known. For Rini to be afraid like that gave her an idea of the depth of his trauma.

An aide helped Rini into the bathroom but stayed outside the door. He clung to the bathroom sink and stared in the mirror. *So I'm Rini Baldasseri, whoever that is.* Rini for short, his alleged wife had interjected. *A mining engineer?* He couldn't fathom any of it.

The only way he could half imagine they'd been married was because she spoke the same language with him when no one else could. Several times he'd studied the photo of them kissing. They'd looked like they were devouring each other. A picture didn't lie about their hunger for each other. Neither did the wedding band and diamond she wore on her ring finger.

She was very, very beautiful. In fact, on a beauty scale of one to ten, his blonde wife with those lagoon-green eyes came out closer to a fifty. They'd been married six months? How was it possible he didn't recognize her or remember her in any way?

The doctor told him he had amnesia. He knew what it meant, but he'd never known anyone who'd had it. Maybe he did, but the amnesia had erased that memory. He simply couldn't believe it was his problem now.

No longer receiving an antibiotic through an IV, he began the task of shaving his beard. The hair on his face itched and drove him crazy. When he'd gotten rid of it, he groaned to see the rest of him. After looking at those pictures, he could tell he'd lost weight.

He wore medical scrubs the other hospital

had lent him. Besides hanging on him, the dull color didn't help his sallow complexion. No shoes. Surgery socks covered his feet.

Well, no more of this!

He stripped down and got into the shower with hot water. Nothing had ever felt so good in his life. But how did he know that? How did he know anything now that twenty-nine years of life had just been wiped from his brain?

Luna would be back in later. She'd promised.

Rini knew he wasn't the same man she'd married, not physically or psychologically. Though she was putting on a good face to be his translator, he couldn't bear the thought that it was possible she pitied him.

He put on the white toweling bathrobe the hospital provided. After reaching for a towel to dry his hair, he walked back into the room. The aide helped him into bed.

The next thing he needed was a haircut. At least he had a picture of his former self. Maybe someone here at the hospital could do the job for him. The sooner he could get back to looking like the man in the photo, the sooner he might recover his memory.

His dinner soon arrived. The smell of hot coffee and lasagna teased his senses, warming his taste buds. He'd never tasted food so wonderful and had finished everything by the time Luna had returned. Though her arms were loaded, he found himself once again noticing her five-foot-seven height and the curves of her womanly figure.

She put two small suitcases on the floor against the wall and walked closer to inspect him. A smile broke out on her stunning face with its high cheekbones. Her luminescent green eyes played over him.

"Wow! What a difference a shave makes."

He wiped his mouth with a napkin. "Good or bad?"

"Never bad, Rini. The hair made you look like a dashing pirate. But I like what you've done."

Her comment improved his mood, relieving him of some of the anxiety building inside him over his incredible situation. "Do you think there's a barber around here?"

"I don't know, but tomorrow I'll ask Emilio, the one who usually cuts your hair, to come to the hospital. How does that sound?"

"I'd be even more indebted to you."

She glanced at his tray. "You ate everything. Do you want more?"

"Since I'm not used to such a big helping, I'm fine for now."

"I'm glad it tasted good to you." She removed the tray and put it on another table. "Your grandparents chose your menu with all the foods you love."

"That was thoughtful of them."

"They love you. Your *nonna* wants to fatten you up." No one wanted that to happen faster than Rini, who was desperate to get back to the man he'd seen in those little photos. "The fact that you're alive has brought them back to life," Luna told him. "They can't do enough for you."

His gaze darted to the suitcases. "What did you bring with you?"

"In one of them are your own toiletries and some clothes for you, including shoes, for when you're released. I'm afraid until then you'll have to wear a hospital gown."

"Let's hope it isn't green."

A smile came and went. "I don't think so. You've lived through a nightmare, Rini, but you're home now."

Home, as in his own home, meant nothing

to him. The realization raised his anxiety level once more. "What's in the other case?"

"A surprise."

"Can I see it now?"

She carried it over and placed it on the end of the bed to open.

"A laptop?"

Her eyes brightened. "It's *your* laptop with all the mining information on it." She pulled it out and set it on his lap. "I'll plug it in." She walked around the bed to find a wall outlet.

Rini's heart pounded. Maybe looking through it would trigger something in his memory. Excited, he turned it on, but there was a prompt to supply the password. He had no idea and his excitement turned to more frustration.

"I'll type it in." As Luna leaned over, a strand of her metallic-blond hair grazed his cheek and he breathed in her fragrance. The delicious smell of strawberries distracted him.

Only then did he notice the icons that had popped up on the screen.

Luna stepped away. "Click anywhere you want, and you'll see photos, maps, charts, everything you want to know about the King Midas Mine. It's your baby," she added with a wink he found intriguing.

He got started, but after ten minutes of going through material he didn't recognize, he closed the lid.

She got the message. "You're tired. Tomorrow you can go through more of it." After unplugging it, she put the laptop back in the suitcase and moved it over against the wall.

Just then one of the female staff came in to take his vital signs and give him more pills to fight the infection.

"Where are you going?" Rini called to Luna after the nurse left.

"I'm staying right here until you fall asleep." She walked toward him and sat down in the chair next to the bed.

And then what? "I don't want you to leave."

"I wouldn't think of it. I'll be sleeping on the couch in the other room of the suite."

He looked around, realizing this hospital room didn't resemble the one at the hospital in Slovenia. Rini hadn't thought about it until this minute. "This is a suite?"

"Yes, with everything you could want, including the best doctors in the world."

Rini rubbed his chest absently. "Why am I being treated like royalty?"

"Because...you're the Crown Prince of San Vitano. When your grandfather passes away, you'll be King of your beautiful country."

His eyes closed tightly in reaction. "He's the King? You're not teasing me, are you?" She'd overloaded him, but Dr. Romano told her to be natural with him.

She got up from the chair. "While you let that sink in, I'll bring you our family album of photos that will prove your heritage beyond doubt."

In a minute she put a large, heavy album in his hands. He looked at her before opening to the first page that showed the royal family in full dress from years earlier. Rini recognized his grandparents but no other members of the family. Slowly, he leafed through each page, bringing the photos up-to-date.

Luna pointed out the picture of Vincenzo to him. It meant nothing.

Rini studied him for a moment, then kept turning the pages. He stopped when he came to the wedding pictures of him and his dazzling bride, Luna. He felt a quickening of his pulse. Rini might not remember her, but his attraction to her was growing stronger by the minute. In the picture she wore a tiara.

He looked up and stared at her. "This means you have to be Princess Baldasseri."

Luna nodded. "I'm a commoner, married to the prince of my dreams."

A grimace marred his features. "I don't recall anything about my life or yours." This time he shut the cover of the album with more force than he'd done the laptop. How in the name of heaven couldn't he remember her?

"You have to give it time, Rini." On that note she took it from him and put it back in the suitcase. "I'll take your toiletries to the bathroom so you can brush your teeth and get ready for bed." She disappeared. When she returned, she said, "There's a hospital gown in there for you, too. You must be exhausted."

"On the contrary, I'm wide-awake," he claimed. "I'm afraid you're the one who should be in bed after this long day. Ask the staff to bring in a cot. The other room is too far away. I want you to sleep by me in case I wake up in the night and need to talk."

He not only needed her near him, he

wanted her near him, too. In truth, he found that he *desired* her. It came as a shock to him.

"Just push the button on the bed, Rini. Someone will come."

Within a minute one of the male staff entered the room. Luna smiled at him. "Could a cot be brought in for me?"

"Of course. I'll see to it housekeeping brings one immediately."

"Thank you."

Rini waited until they were alone. "I'll be right back, Luna." He got out of bed to head for the bathroom. Inside he discovered the things she'd brought. He opened the new toothbrush and got busy, then took off his robe and slipped on the hospital gown. When Rini did emerge, he knew he looked a far cry from the prince of her dreams.

# CHAPTER FOUR

AFTER HOUSEKEEPING ARRIVED and turned down the main lights, Luna went in the other room to change into a pair of pale blue running pants and top. When she was ready, she walked back in his room and climbed under the covers of the cot set up next to Rini's bed.

To think that after ten days of grieving for her beloved, he was alive, and they were together under miraculous circumstances. She said a prayer of gratitude and vowed never to let him out of her sight again. It thrilled her that he wanted her to sleep near him. If he only knew how much she adored him, how much she'd missed their lovemaking.

When she'd finished her prayers, she turned on her side to face him and realized he'd already gotten into his bed and was looking down at her.

"I see tears," he murmured. "Am I so hideous?"

"Oh, Rini—" she cried out in pain, wiping them with the back of her hand. "These are tears of thanksgiving that you didn't die! I'm still trying to absorb the horrendous experience you've endured while we all th-thought—"

"I was dead?" he broke in. "To be honest, I prayed for oblivion every time I woke up to another day of endless hell, not knowing who I was or where I came from."

She rose up on one elbow. "But you know now, and I'm here to help you for as long as it takes."

His black brows furrowed. "I might never get my memory back," he said in a gravelly tone of voice. "Considering that we're married, have you thought of what that means?"

It was all she'd been thinking about. The possibility that he might never remember anything made her too ill to think about right now. "I'd rather we took this one step at a time. Yesterday morning I woke up to face another day without you. Before the morning was out, I'd flown to Rezana to find out any information I could. Then I found out you were alive!"

"Drugged was more like it," he muttered with irony.

Shades of the old Rini made her smile. "Yet, after you woke up in the hospital, I discovered you could understand and speak Romansh when you hadn't understood any other language.

"Can you have any idea how I felt? I didn't know you could only speak Romansh. My love for you came pouring out, and suddenly you opened your eyes because you understood me. I thought I'd die for joy!"

He moved closer to the edge of his bed. "When I heard your voice say, 'I love you,' I thought an angel was speaking to me. In all that horrific time, those were the only words that I understood. It wouldn't be possible for you to understand how I felt. In that moment there was a connection between us. I didn't remember you, but you became my lodestone to cling to. It was an answer to my anguish I never thought I'd receive."

"From your wife, no less," she quipped. "If two miracles can happen in one day, who knows how many more are in store? What I want to know is why the other hospital didn't send any of your things with you?"

"Things?" He sounded incredulous.

"Your clothes and wallet. Your boots. Where are your watch and wedding ring?"

He actually let out a dry laugh, the first she'd heard come out of him. "You'd have to have been there to understand."

She sat straight up. "Tell me. I want to know everything."

"First things first." His gaze wandered over her. "What are you wearing?"

"Oh—my running pants and top."

"Have you always worn them to bed?"

Heat swamped her cheeks. "No. But I brought these because we're around other people."

"What do you normally wear to bed?"

Honesty was vital between them. "A nightgown, but it never lasts long."

He thought about it. "What do *I* usually wear?"

"Nothing once your robe comes off."

A frown marred his handsome features. "How come I didn't get you pregnant?"

"Oh, Rini." She laughed. "We talked about having a family right away and decided not to use protection. I couldn't wait to have babies with you."

Rini rubbed the side of his smoothly shaven jaw. "Were you worried about it when conception didn't happen?"

It *did* happen, but this was one piece of information her husband wasn't ready for yet. They needed to get closer to each other before she told him he was going to be a father.

"Six months is such a short time to be married, don't you think?"

"You're right. Was I upset about it?"

"No, but we both hoped I'd get pregnant soon."

He rose up and dangled his powerful legs over the side of the bed. "We didn't sleep together before our wedding?"

She smiled. "We only dated six weeks before marrying. You told me you wanted me to be your wife before you made love to me. We were both in a hurry. Your grandparents were shocked that you proposed to me so fast. They'd hoped you would marry a certain princess from Rome."

"So it would have been an arranged marriage?"

"Yes."

"Did I know her well?"

"You avoided the subject of marriage as much as possible."

"So what are you saying about us?"

She flashed him a smile. "The moment we met we knew we were in love. That was it, and you broke off with her. You told me you were never in love with her and I believed you. Otherwise, how could we explain what happened to us?"

He eyed her for a quiet moment. "Were my grandparents upset?"

"If they were, they hid it well and allowed you to marry me, a woman of the people. That's something no other royal has ever done in your bloodline. From what I understood, you often defied convention, but you are your own person and your grandparents' favorite."

At this point he got off the bed and started pacing, then stopped. "What happened to my parents?"

"They died in a boating accident in a ferocious storm four years ago on Lake Diamanti on the outskirts of Asteria. I'm so sorry and wished I could have met them."

He moved closer to her. "What about your parents?"

"They died when I was two in a plane accident, so I don't remember them. I was raised by my grandparents. My grandfather managed a bank. They died separately of pneumonia. I ended up getting my degree in business administration from the University of St. Gallen in Switzerland. I worked later, but didn't find satisfaction, so I applied for jobs elsewhere, even outside the country.

"Being bilingual in Italian as well as Romansh, I was able to interview at the Baldasseri Gold Mining Corporation here in San Vitano. Fabio Machetto, the office manager, offered me a position. I liked the staff and atmosphere and felt I could be happy there.

"Two weeks later you came into the office. I fell so hard for you it was embarrassing."

His hands went to his hips. "Apparently, that worked both ways."

"Yes, thank heaven! My grandparents would have loved you. As for the rest, you and I started to speak Romansh and you took me to lunch. From that time on we were inseparable."

"What about other boyfriends?" he rapped out, as if he couldn't take in the information fast enough.

"I dated some, but meeting you altered my universe. Now, enough about me. I've answered your questions and want you to tell me why you were sent in the helicopter without your belongings."

She heard a sharp intake of breath before Rini got back into his bed, stretching out before turning to her. "As I told Doctor Romano, I tripped and fell on the side of the highway. A kind man drove me to the hospital, but I don't remember what happened. Maybe someone came by before he did and stripped me of everything. When I was dressed in hospital scrubs, they probably threw my clothes away. I don't know. No one in there spoke my language, or I theirs."

Luna groaned. "But the contents of your wallet would have told someone everything."

"Maybe I lost it in the cave-in. Once in that hospital, I figured that one day I wouldn't wake up. I prayed for that eventuality."

"Instead, the policeman, Zigo, helped me find you," she blurted. "If it hadn't been for

him, I would never have found you. I plan
to do something wonderful for him."

"We'll find a way to do it, Luna. I'll want
to reward the doctor, too."

"Of course, we will. Carlo Bruni, the man
who came with me, is your grandfather's
foreign emissary. He was responsible for ar-
ranging everything. Carlo is one of our favorite people."

For a minute quiet reigned. Luna lay back
on the cot, wishing they shared a bed. She
ached to hold him in her arms and love them
both into oblivion.

"Are you going to sleep on me?" The deep
voice she loved sounded close to accusatory.

"No." She smiled. "I thought you had nodded off."

"Anything but. Tell me where we live."

Luna turned to him in the semidarkness.
"Our home is a lovely, spacious *palazzo* not
far from the royal palace. You were born and
raised there. It has fruit trees in the back.
When they blossom, it looks like fairyland.
We have a housekeeper, Viola, who's also
the cook. She's married to the caretaker,
Mateo. Both have been with you for close
to fifteen years now."

"Do I have friends?"

"You and your second cousin, Vincenzo, are good friends, but with him running the timber business in Scuol, neither of you see each other as often as you'd like."

"That's it?"

"Since you and I met, I'm afraid we haven't socialized that much with other people. I only met him at our wedding. As it is, you have to squeeze in your royal duties with your mining concerns.

"Since the quake, Vincenzo has taken over some of your royal duties. He's your grandfather's grandnephew. He's always had a great relationship with him. Your whole family is very close. Needless to say, you and Vincenzo have been like brothers."

She heard the rustling of his sheets. "Speaking of brothers, if mine hadn't died, *he'd* be the Crown Prince."

"That's true."

Rini let out a frustrated sigh. "How soon can I get out of here?"

He'd grown restless. This was obviously too much information for one day.

"After your tests tomorrow, you'll have your first session with Doctor Tullia. Then the barber will come, and Doctor Romano will make his rounds. You can negotiate with him."

"Am I that impossible?" he asked in a dry tone.

"The hospital record in Rezana indicated you're a tour de force."

"In other words, I'm out of control."

"Not at all. Let's just say you have a convincing way about you."

"That's the definition of a tyrant."

"Hardly, Rini. You're a man who knows what he wants and goes after it."

"Come hell or high water?"

"I'll let you decide. According to Doctor Miakar, you're manageable if you're given time to think about it. I'd say that sums you up very nicely. Now, you need to sleep. I'll see you tomorrow after your first session with Doctor Tullia. *Buna notg*, Rini."

Rini wasn't ready to call it a night, but his wife had other ideas and turned on her side away from him. The clock on the wall said 1:40 a.m. After the day Luna had lived through in order to find him, it shouldn't have surprised him she'd just passed out on him.

Without her, he knew he would have eventually died in Rezana.

To realize that she'd followed her gut instinct to discover if he was still alive had humbled him so deeply, his body shook with sobs. He buried his face in the pillow, needing no convincing that he was married to the most exceptional, courageous wife he could imagine. And exceptionally desirable.

He went over the things she'd told him about their marriage. They'd taken vows within six weeks? Incredible. He'd married a beauty, but it came from her soul, too. Obviously, they'd been so close, they hadn't wanted or needed other people.

But before falling asleep, something had started to disturb him. He planned to bring it up with the therapist Dr. Romano had told him about.

The next day when he was brought back to his room following his tests and had gotten into bed, to his surprise a younger man entered the room with Dr. Tullia. He introduced himself as Chispar, bilingual in Italian and Romansh. "I teach at the college here and have been sent by the head to offer temporary assistance to Doctor Tullia."

Rini didn't like it that Luna hadn't come to this session. For that matter, she'd already left the hospital when he'd awakened. He'd felt abandoned. "Where's my wife?"

Chispar explained there would be other times when the doctor wanted her there, but not for this first session. All Rini could do was accept the situation and they got started.

It was a strange experience because he'd thought Dr. Tullia would ask him a lot of questions. Instead, he said, "Rini? Doctor Romano tells me you've been told you have amnesia and understand the meaning of the word. Do you feel well enough to talk?"

Chispar translated.

Rini had to believe his wife knew about this and decided he'd better cooperate. Otherwise, it would be reported that he was "unmanageable."

After Rini nodded, the two men pulled up chairs by him and sat down. Dr. Tullia appeared relaxed. "Memory loss affects people differently. Everything from frustration to fear. Why don't you tell me what you want to talk about?"

"I feel fine and want to get out of here. How soon can I go home?"

"Do you know where home is?"

"My wife has explained where we live."

"You're comfortable with her?"

"She found me. If she didn't like me, I assume she wouldn't have come looking for me."

"It sounds as if you trust her."

"I don't believe she has lied to me, but—"

"But what?"

"She's been like a saint."

"Explain that word."

"You know. Perfect. In every way."

"And that disturbs you?"

"Hell, yes. How do I know that beneath her facade she…pities me and really doesn't want me to go home with her?"

He pondered the question. "How do you know she pities you? Has she told you that?"

"No."

"Then maybe you need to discuss that with her privately. It sounds like you are putting your own feelings on to her."

Rini let out an exasperated groan.

Dr. Tullia sat forward. "Rini, from what I've heard about you, you are a powerful, confident man. Even if your memory doesn't return, let's work on getting your confidence back.

"Under the circumstances I'll tell Doctor Romano I feel fine about letting you go home with your wife. Until he sees fit to release you, I'll arrange a session with you every morning here. After you leave I'll want to talk to you twice a week in my office here at the hospital for the next four weeks. You'll always be able to call me at home or the office anytime if an emergency should arise, even in the middle of the night."

Rini felt relieved when both men got up and said goodbye.

No sooner had they left than another man close to Rini's age and tall like him came into his hospital room. He wore sporty clothes, nothing like the hospital staff. He had brilliant blue eyes and dark brown hair in a style worn much like Rini's in the photo of him. For once it was someone he thought he recognized.

The other man studied him for an overly long moment that made him uncomfortable. "You'll never know how good it is to see you," he said in Romansh.

After hearing the familiar language spoken to him, Rini got it. This was his second cousin. "I take it you are Vincenzo."

A broad smile broke out on his handsome face. "Give this man the prize! Was Luna just spoofing me? You haven't really lost your memory, have you, *cusregna*?"

This surprise visit from his Romansh-speaking royal cousin made him uncomfortable. He couldn't comprehend being royal or the Crown Prince. In fact, he didn't want to think about it. "Afraid so. She showed me a picture of you in our family album."

The smile slowly faded, and Vincenzo sat down by him. "I'm here to be of help in any way that I can."

"I appreciate that, but I have my wife."

Vincenzo leaned forward with his hands clasped between his legs. "I know that. She's the angel who found you. But your grandfather called me last night and explained that you need a translator while you're in the hospital."

"Doctor Tullia brought a man from the college with him who speaks Romansh."

"Understood. But if you need it for other reasons, I'm available."

"Luna told me you've taken over the duties of Crown Prince. I also understand you're engaged to be married. You don't have the time to do anything else."

"I have time for you. She lives in Italy and understands I need to be with you."

His anxiety crept up on him. "Where is Luna?"

"I have no idea. That's why I'm here. To fill in for her and give her some space. My grandfather told me your grandparents are worried about both of you."

Did Luna want space? Had she already told the family that? His fear that she might not want him to go with her grew worse.

"Tell me what you want or need, Rini. I'll do whatever I can."

Rini didn't question the man's sincerity. He saw it in his eyes and heard it in his expression. But he still couldn't handle much more of this. The life of a royal was anathema to him, even if it would offend them if he expressed the sentiment. It was the last job on earth he could imagine wanting. He needed to talk to Dr. Tullia. Right now he didn't want another person from the family involved in his life, no matter how well-meaning. The thought was making him ill.

"Luna says you run a timber business?"

"Yes, but your welfare is much more important to me. When I arrived at the palace, Carlo Bruno was there and told me about your beautiful wife and all she went through to find you. There's a woman who lives by faith. She believed you were alive. How remarkable is that? I swear if my fiancée turns out to be a wife as wonderful as Luna, I'll think I have died and gone to heaven."

"I can tell you mean that, Vincenzo, so I have thought of one important thing you could do for me."

"Name it."

"Luna has explained to me what my princely duties consisted of before all of this happened to me. From what I've gathered, my grandfather has started to rely on you. Since I can't be the person he used to depend on, I'm glad you're the one he's looking to now."

Vincenzo shook his head. "Your condition isn't permanent, Rini."

"Maybe it is."

"But it couldn't be. Some of my friends who've had ski accidents have suffered memory loss, but it always comes back.

Now that you're getting expert medical care, you're going to be back to normal in no time."

"That's where you're wrong, Vincenzo. Doctor Romano says I have a unique case called a fugue state. My amnesia is very different, and I mustn't expect it to ever come back."

His cousin's expression changed to one of shock. "I don't believe it. I bet Luna doesn't believe it, either."

"I'm afraid she's starting to. We're both doing everything we can to accept that our situation is permanent. My grandfather needs to accept it, too. I'm no longer able to fulfill my formal function in the monarchy. Therefore, by royal right, the role of Crown Prince has fallen to you. One day you'll be ruling San Vitano."

Vincenzo shot up from the chair and started pacing. Then he wheeled around to face Rini. "Does your grandfather know how you feel?"

"Not yet. But he will. That's why I'm depending on you. I won't need a translator when I'm released. While I'm here for the next few days, Doctor Tullia has this college teacher to serve as a translator for me. When I'm released, I'll have Luna."

"We all assumed you had temporary amnesia, Rini."

"I hoped the same thing, but it's not going to happen. Luna tells me my grandfather needs a man he can mold to be King. She says the family sings your praises and I take her word for it."

Vincenzo's blue eyes glinted from moisture. "You would have made a great king, Rini. I idolized you and still do for the way you're handling your affliction now."

"I'm trying to handle it, and I'm glad we've talked. I can't be the Crown Prince. I don't have any conception of what that would be like. I'm only glad that you are the designated one now. That's a burden I willingly throw off without knowing anything about it. I wish you the joy of it. Does your fiancée have any idea you're going to be King of San Vitano one day?"

"Yes."

"Tell me about her."

"She's Princess Valentina Di Fiore Visconti of Padua, the daughter of Count Giuseppe Visconti."

"None of that means a thing to me."

"I know. I'm so sorry."

"I've discovered it's life. I was the only survivor of a quake that killed seven other men. For ten days I lay in the hospital, wondering if I would live to see another day."

Vincenzo just stood there and shook his head.

"One thing I *have* learned. My grandparents are good people."

"They're wonderful. You have no idea how much they love and admire you."

"Luna tells me they have great faith in you. It's a worry off my mind if you're helping them because I can't."

"Understood. What will you do?"

Rini lifted his head. "Ask me in a year and maybe I'll be able to tell you."

"Is there anything I can do for you before I go back to the palace?"

"If you see Luna, ask her to come ASAP."

Vincenzo nodded and started to leave.

Rini called to him. "Thank you for coming and being willing to help me. Luna said you and I were best friends. I believe it and wish you well."

The visit from his cousin had relieved him

of a burden, but it had also made him antsy. He got up and walked over to the window, wondering what had happened to his wife.

While he was thinking about her, he heard her voice at the door. He swung around as she walked in. She looked stunning in a pale pink matching blouse and skirt. Another strange man had come in with her, carrying a small satchel. "Rini? Good afternoon. This is your barber, Emilio."

"*Buona sera*, Your Highness."

# CHAPTER FIVE

RINI STARED AT his wife, who'd taught his barber how to say good afternoon in Romansh. "Tell Emilio I'm impressed." He reached over to the side table. "Will you hand him this photo and ask him to make me look like I did here? He may have forgotten."

"I doubt it." Luna grinned and walked over to take it from him.

He recognized the strawberry scent and was haunted by her fragrance. She showed the photo to Emilio. The two of them spoke in Italian. It frustrated Rini that he couldn't understand them and determined to learn Italian ASAP.

She lifted her head. Her hair gleamed a golden white. "He says he finds your disheveled hair an interesting change. Are you sure you don't want to create a new style?"

"Positive!"

"Then he wants you to get out of bed. Come and sit in the chair by the table." She cocked her head. "Can I watch, or is this a private male thing? I've never gone to the barber with you."

"Stay with me."

"All right." She pulled the chair out for him while Emilio emptied his bag on the table and picked up the shears and trimmer. Luna sat down in another chair to watch. "How did it go with Vincenzo?"

"I like him. I also fired him from the job of being my translator and asked him to work with my grandfather."

Wow. "Well, that says it all." She smiled at him.

At this point Emilio got busy. "Tell Rini I can see the place on the crown of his head where he was hurt. It's healed but tell him to treat that area gently when he brushes his hair."

Luna translated. "Does it still hurt, Rini?"

"It's a little tender if I press on it. Doctor Romano said it would fade with time."

"Thank goodness."

Before long Emilio used an edger before

he declared success. The barber looked at Rini with satisfaction before handing him a small mirror. "Take a look."

She translated while Rini compared the image in the mirror to the picture he held.

Rini nodded and handed back the mirror. His gaze swerved to Luna. "Tell him I can't complain."

"He's paid you a great compliment, Emilio," she said in Italian.

*"Sì?"*

*"Sì.* Rini thinks you did a great job."

A smile broke out on his face. "It's been a pleasure to serve you as usual." He gathered up his things, said goodbye to Luna and left.

Rini watched him go, glad the two of them were finally alone. He got to his feet. "What does my wife think now?"

Her dreamy green eyes studied him. She walked over and kissed his cheek. "You smell good and look like my old Rini."

"You always smell wonderful," he murmured, wanting to reach out and crush her to him. But he didn't dare. Not yet. First, he'd get in shape and regain the weight he'd lost. He wasn't about to forget she'd fallen in love with his former self.

Luna smiled. "Welcome home eleven days late."

"That's where I want to go. Doctor Tullia said he'd tell Doctor Romano he felt fine about releasing me."

"How wonderful!" Her instant response went a long way to reassure him it was good news to her. He saw no shadow. "The morning you left to inspect the mine was the first time we'd ever been apart." Her throat closed up. "I'd planned a special anniversary dinner for that evening when you got home." She'd apparently planned another surprise, too.

"When your grandparents came to the *palazzo* with the news there'd been an earthquake and men were trapped in the mine, including my beloved husband—I thought I would die."

He heard the pain in her voice. It caught him unawares. As his gaze fused with hers, one of the staff chose that moment to bring in two dinner trays and put them on the table. Luna turned to thank the woman, breaking the trance that held them.

Once they were alone, she invited Rini to sit back down and eat with her. "Um… Your grandmother knows how much you love veal cooked in wine. I love it, too. This *osso bucco* looks tantalizing."

If anything looked tantalizing, it was Luna.

He started eating. "Does our cook make meals like this?"

"Much better, actually. You'll love her *bruschetta*."

Good. He'd gain weight fast and begin to look like the man she'd married.

"Do you cook, Luna?"

"Not well, but *you* do when we eat outside on the back patio."

He put his fork down. "Are you joking with me?"

"Not at all. Your specialty is either grilled swordfish or salmon on a stick with your own signature lemon sauce. I understand you learned the recipes from your mother, who was reported to be a fabulous cook. Three days after we went to lunch, you invited me to the *palazzo*. To my surprise you barbecued our dinner and I knew I was in love."

"How soon did I propose?"

"That night after you drove me back to my pitiful apartment."

"So fast?"

She nodded. "I told you I'd give you my answer after our third date, which was two days later. I wanted to impress you with *my* cooking, which turned out to be a flop because the oven broke down. Raw chicken wasn't what I had in mind. You laughed and said nothing else mattered as long as I would agree to marry you."

He eyed her intently. "How long did you make me wait for your answer?"

"I didn't. I was shameless and told you I'd envisioned you as my husband when we went to lunch. You pulled a ring out of your shirt pocket and put it on my ring finger."

Luna extended her left hand with its engagement ring and wedding band. He gripped her hand and studied the three-carat diamond set in gold. "I can see I had good taste."

"In everything!" she cried. "You told me the gold in both rings came from the Baldasseri gold mine and were fashioned expressly for me. Inside the gold band you'd had words engraved: *Rini and Luna forever.* You'll never know what that night meant to me. At first, I thought I must be dreaming, but from then on we spent every free moment together and I'd never been so happy in my life. But if you want to know the truth, when I found you alive at the hospital in Rezana, *that* was the most thrilling, glorious moment of my life. You weren't lost to me after all." Her voice trembled. "You just can't know what finding you meant to me."

He stirred in the chair. "I know what it meant to hear a feminine voice say I love you. At that moment I knew I wasn't going to die, that I'd been saved."

*"Rini—"*

He rubbed his thumb against her palm the way he used to do as a prelude to making love. Her husband might have lost his memory, but his body reacted the same way it did before the quake. His touch brought her alive.

Luna slowly removed her hand from Rini's and sat back. The feel of him had sent tingles of longing through her body that wouldn't go away. But maybe she'd revealed too much of herself to him. What had she been thinking? He didn't know her from Adam!

She'd wanted to tell him as much as she could about their married life together. But she'd been an open book about her personal feelings for him. It might be a turnoff if she went too far. She adored him whether he'd lost his memory or not and wanted their marriage to last forever. However, could she say the same thing for him?

In his eyes Luna was a total stranger to him. In revealing her heart, he might be feeling suffocated. Though he'd said he was anxious to go home, he had no idea what that meant. She could understand his wanting to get out of the hospital. It had to be a kind of jail to him. Naturally, he craved his independence. Unfortunately for him, he needed her help to communicate.

She wouldn't blame him if he preferred someone like Chispar to stay at the *palazzo* with them, but that was the last thing she wanted. Under the circumstances it would be better if she didn't go to work at the mining office for a while.

Luna would discuss this with Dr. Tullia. Maybe he would tell her it would be a good idea if someone else was there on weekdays with whom he had no emotional ties. It might make his life much easier while he tried to adapt to a new life. But she didn't want to be apart from him for a minute.

Later, when Dr. Romano came in for his evening rounds accompanied by Chispar, he explained he wanted to examine his patient. Luna translated for Rini. "I promise I'll be back after he leaves."

She walked to the sitting room of the suite to phone Dr. Tullia, who'd given her his card. He didn't answer, so she left the message for him to call her. Hoping he would get back to her before bed, she changed into her running pants and top in the en-suite bathroom. While she was brushing her teeth, her cell rang.

She wiped her mouth and checked the caller ID before clicking on. "Doctor Tullia? Thank you for calling me back. I'm so grateful."

"I'm here for you and Rini. Tell me what's wrong."

"*I'm* the problem tonight."

"Go on."

She told him about her latest concerns. "I love my husband and let him know we were madly in love from the very beginning. But he has no memory of me, and maybe it has put too much pressure on him. What if he really doesn't want to go home with me? What if he'd like some space and Chispar could be home with him while I'm at work? What do you think?"

"Let me ask you a question. Knowing that he might never remember you, do you want him to love you the same as before?"

"Yes!" she cried. "He's my *raison d'être*."

"Then here's my advice. Do exactly what your instincts have been telling you to say and do. Don't hold back. Continue to be yourself. Ask him if he wants company when you're at work. In time you'll know if he feels nonreceptive or smothered."

"That's what worries me. *How* will I know?"

"Is there any doubt in your mind that he'll tell you? Your husband is assertive and doesn't keep his thoughts to himself."

She chuckled. "You're right about that."

"Some things about human nature don't change, do they?"

"I can't thank you enough for your advice, Doctor. You've made me feel better."

"Good. I'm here for you anytime. Good night, Luna."

They hung up and she left the bathroom to find Dr. Romano in the sitting room waiting for her. She hurried over to him. Chispar had left. "How is he tonight?"

"He's coming along well. I'd feared he might have stomach problems getting used to regular meals, but he assured me he's hungry and eating everything. At this rate he'll gain back the weight he lost without problem."

"That's my grandmother-in-law's fault. She's planned all his favorite dishes."

He smiled. "Well, it's showing. I guess you're aware he wants to leave."

"Yes. I can tell he's restless."

"He needs to stay in the hospital two more days while he undergoes more tests and works with the physiotherapist. I'll put in orders to release him on Thursday morning. He's in good shape considering what he's been through. Call me if you have any questions."

"I have one more. Will he be able to drive after he goes home?"

"We don't know, but I'm sure you'll find out. Again, let him be the one to decide."

"Of course. Good night, Doctor. Thank you for everything you've done."

"We're all thankful the Prince survived."

Luna walked him to the entrance before heading straight for Rini's room.

"Hi! I'm back." She wanted to fling herself into his arms.

He eyed her thoroughly. It sent shivers of delight down her spine. "I thought you'd never come." His voice sounded more like a growl. She could believe he'd actually missed her.

"Oh, ye of little faith." She moved the cot away from the wall and laid it out near Rini's bed. "Before I get in, shall I turn on the TV?"

"Is that what we used to do?"

"Sometimes we watched the news or a film. Does a movie interest you? We could pick something easily understandable even if you can't follow the language."

She could feel his penetrating gray eyes appraise her. It made her heart beat so fast she could hardly breathe. "I think I'd rather talk and find out what Doctor Romano had to say to you."

Was he worried? She turned off the overhead light and climbed into her cot to face him. He lay on his side with his head slightly elevated. His eyes never left her face.

"Do you want the good or the bad news first?"

"How am I supposed to answer that?" His hand had gripped the sheet in reaction. She shouldn't have said it. His tension was too severe.

Luna sat up in the cot. "Rini—I was only kidding. It's all good. You can go home on Thursday."

He rubbed his jaw absently. "Not till then?" She heard his disappointment.

"That's only two more days while he runs a few more tests."

"Will I be free to do anything? Like fly?"

Had she heard him right? "You mean like travel on a jet?"

"I want a chopper to fly me to Rezana so I can thank the police officer for listening to you and telling you where to find me."

"So do I. We'll do something for the doctor, too."

She adored her husband, who wanted to repay the people who'd helped him. His humanity was well-known among the mining community, even if he didn't realize it. "Maybe you could talk to your grandfather and find a way to gift Doctor Miakar in a meaningful way."

His gaze narrowed on her. "That's an idea."

Already, he was focusing on others, sounding more and more like her husband. She took a deep breath. "I'd love to go with you."

"I wouldn't go anywhere without you, Luna."

He sounded like he meant it, but was it only because she was his link to communication? "Rini, tomorrow will you ask Doctor Romano if you'll be under any restrictions about flying in a plane or helicopter?"

"I will." He lowered the head of the bed and rearranged his pillow but couldn't get it right. "I also need to learn Italian so I can talk to him myself."

"Agreed." Incredible that Rini had spoken it from birth. It was there in his brain somewhere. "I'll give you your first lesson tonight if you want. Many words in Romansh have a slight similarity to Italian. You'll learn it in no time."

"Try me."

Delighted he wanted a lesson, she said, "Let's go with some simple words. Say *ciao*. It means *hello*."

He answered with perfect inflection.

"*Bene*. That means *good*, or it can mean *well*. Say it."

"*Bene.*"

"Now try *buongiorno*. It means *good morning*."

He responded perfectly.

"*Excellente*, Rini. Now two more phrases. *Come va?* It means *how are you*?"

"*Come va?*" he experimented several times.

"*Bravo!*" she cried when he reproduced it correctly.

He rose up. "Are you sure you aren't a schoolteacher?"

Luna laughed. "I promise."

"You make a good one. This is fun." That comment thrilled her heart.

"Then let's keep going. When someone asks you that question and you answer it, then you say *E tu?* It means *And you*?"

"*E tu?*"

"*Sì*. That means *yes*. You make a wonderful Italian parrot."

A deep laugh broke from him, the first

she'd heard since finding him. This was a magical moment. "All right. Now, let's have conversation number one. Here we go. *Ciao*, Rini Baldasseri."

He sat up. "*Ciao*, Luna Baldasseri."

"*Come va?*"

"*Bene. E tu?*"

"*Bene.*"

She clapped her hands. "That was *perfetto*. You sounded totally Italian and are such a good student, it's scary. Now, let's have conversation number two."

"I'll start it," he offered. His eyes were alive with light.

"Go ahead."

"*Buongiorno*, Luna Baldasseri."

"*Buongiorno*, Rinieri Francesco Baldasseri."

He frowned. "Rinieri? Where did that name come from?"

"That's your full name in honor of King Rinieri Umberto Baldasseri, your great-great-great-grandfather."

"No wonder you call me Rini."

She smiled.

"What's *your* full name?"

"Luna Biancho Baldasseri."

"Biancho… Biancho…" he said several times.

"You sound pure Italian, but I think that's enough lesson for now except to learn the word for good-night. It's *buona notte.*"

"*Buona notte,*" he repeated. "But I don't want to go to sleep yet."

She took that as a compliment. "I think it's one of the most beautiful words in Italian, Rini. Now, I'm sure you're exhausted even if you don't realize it. I know I am."

"*Buona notte,* Luna."

"*Buona notte, tesoro mio.*"

He cocked his head. "What did you just say?"

Uh-oh. Heat flooded her cheeks. She'd married a brilliant man and could hear Dr. Tullia telling her to do what came instinctively. "*Tesoro mio.*"

"Are you going to leave me in suspense?" His voice resonated through her insides.

"It's an expression I often used with you." She lay back and closed her eyes tightly.

"And?" he prodded, not willing to let it go. "What does it mean?"

"My treasure."

"Say it again."

*"Tesoro mio."*

After a slight pause she heard him say, "What did I sometimes call you?"

*"Pulcina mia."*

He said it several times. "What does it mean?"

"My little chick."

A low chuckle came out of him. "How do I say *thank you*?"

*"Grazie."*

*"Grazie, pulcina mia. Buon anotte."*

"You know something, Rini? I think you're a fraud. Listening to you right now, no one would guess you'd lost your ability to speak Italian. Before we were married, your grandfather took me aside and told me you were one of the most intelligent men he'd ever known. When the time came for you to rule, you'd be the greatest of the San Vitano kings."

She heard his covers rustle. "I have no idea what the future holds for me, but I'd rather be dead than be a king."

"How do you know that?"

"I just do."

Ooh. She buried her face in the pillow so he couldn't hear her groan. Where had that thought come from? Had it always been buried in his psyche?

Throughout their marriage he'd never expressed negative feelings about being royal. He'd loved his grandfather and had admired him. With few complaints Rini had managed to balance his princely duties with his career as a mining engineer. He hadn't let them intrude on the glorious time they'd had together as man and wife.

The one time she hadn't wanted him to leave for work and felt it was an intrusion was the day of the earthquake. Her body trembled to remember the horror of learning he'd been buried in the debris.

*Don't think about it*, she lectured herself. *Rini's alive and here in the same room with you. We'll be going home in a couple of days.*

Thursday morning Luna awakened and noticed Rini was still out for the count. That was because on the past two nights he'd awakened and got out of bed, too restless to sleep. She feared he'd had nightmares.

Taking care to be quiet, she got up and left the room to change into her skirt and blouse. Once dressed, she went back in Rini's room and put the suitcase in his bathroom. Today he would be able to wear normal clothes home.

She found her purse. After phoning her driver to come and get her, she left the suite. Out in the hall she told the staff at the nursing station she was leaving. "I'll be back to drive my husband home once he's released."

"Plan on ten o'clock and pull up to the ER entrance."

"I'll be there."

On the way home she phoned Leonardo and Antonia to tell them her plans. "I'll call you after he's settled, and we'll go from there." She'd kept in daily touch with them but couldn't tell them to come over yet. Rini needed to express a desire to see them.

A few minutes later she entered the *palazzo*. "Viola?"

"I'm here." The housekeeper hurried to the foyer.

"Rini will be coming home this morning."

The older woman pressed her hands to her mouth with excitement. "The news is out that he's alive and back in San Vitano. It's a day of celebration! Signor Machetti says the office is flooded with hundreds of calls."

Luna nodded. "I don't doubt it."

A pained expression crossed over her face. "He still doesn't remember anything?"

"No, but I've told him about you and Mateo. Would you ask him to do a favor for me?" She nodded. "Ask him to run to the store and buy a supply of protein shakes. Rini needs calories to put on weight and your cooking will do the rest."

Viola beamed. "I'll tell Mateo now and make sure everything gets done."

"You're an angel. I'm going to shower and change. Then I'll be taking his car to get him."

She dashed up the stairs, so excited to be bringing him home she could hardly stand it.

In a few minutes she left the shower to blow-dry her hair and do her makeup. Last Sunday she'd looked like a pale wraith. This morning the color was back in her cheeks. She wore her favorite lipstick and used some eyeliner.

Next, she drew a short-sleeved outfit from the wardrobe that Rini loved on her. He said the green stripes on the white jacket were the color of her eyes. She matched it with a white skirt and white sandals. The green peridot earrings he'd given her on their one-month anniversary complemented her outfit. He might not remember her, but she planned to do everything she could to make herself attractive to him.

Though it was only nine-thirty, she hurried out the back of the *palazzo* to the parking area for the car. Just knowing she'd be bringing him home had made her eager and breathless. First, however, she stopped at a phone store to buy him a new cell phone and installed an app that would be of great help to him. Luna wanted to surprise Rini tonight before they went to bed.

# CHAPTER SIX

RINI HAD LIVED for Thursday to come, but when he awakened, he discovered his appealing wife had disappeared on him. Where in heaven had she gone on this day of all days?

He had to fight his disappointment. Before falling asleep the night before, he'd worked out a conversation to have with her when he said good morning to her. Now it would have to wait, and it frustrated him no end.

After the staff checked his vital signs and he'd eaten breakfast, he went into the bathroom. To his surprise he found the suitcase and opened the lid. She'd packed a dark blue crewneck shirt and a pair of tan pants. There was also a belt. Like he'd told Dr. Tullia, Luna was part angel. He forgave her for slipping away so early.

Stuck in one of the holders he found a pair of darker tan leather sandals. Real shoes after all this time. These were clothes he'd worn before the mine cave-in. He dressed quickly after a shower and shave, deciding to leave the shirt out.

One of the male staff had come into the room with a wheelchair. Behind him Rini saw Dr. Tullia, an unexpected surprise.

*"Ciao, Dottore."*

The doctor lit up with a smile. *"Ciao*, Rini." *"Come va?"*

The man looked shocked. *"Molto bene. E tu?"*

*"Bene."* But Rini lifted his shirt to show the doctor he'd had to tighten the belt a bit. Dr. Tullia broke into laughter. It felt good to communicate on his own with a man he'd started to trust.

Luna had taught him well, otherwise the therapist wouldn't have kept smiling as he patted the wheelchair, indicating Rini should sit down. The other man gathered up the suitcase with his things and the three of them left the suite.

*"Buongiorno!"* Rini called out to the cluster of staff at the nursing station. He received

several greetings back. They clapped and cheered him with bravos.

*"Grazie."*

The staff nodded in understanding before he was wheeled to the elevator. Before long they arrived on the main floor and he was pushed down the hall. He saw the sign *Ingresso di Emergenza*. More than ever, he needed to learn to speak and write Italian quickly.

He felt his pulse pick up speed as they approached the doors. Where was Luna? All of a sudden, he spotted a sleek black sports car drive up.

In the next instant a drop-dead gorgeous blonde woman got out of the driver's seat and walked toward him in the hot sun.

Luna! His heart raced at the sight of her. He was so hooked on her he couldn't think or talk. Her white skirt swung around her long, elegant legs. She drew closer. The green jewels of her earrings couldn't match the dazzling color of those eyes he'd loved looking into. Her exquisite features took his breath.

*"Ciao, tesoro mio."*

His mouth went dry. This wife of his was

beyond wonderful. No wonder he'd proposed to her in less than a week.

"Rini?" she prodded him. He saw concern in her eyes. *"Come va?"*

He was so overcome with the endearment he couldn't swallow. Finally, he said, *"Bene,* now that you're here. I missed seeing you leave this morning."

"You were sleeping so soundly. I didn't want to waken you."

She smiled at Dr. Tullia and thanked him and the other man. Rini watched her press something on the remote she was holding. She told them to put his small suitcase in the cargo space in back, then she looked down at him. Switching to Romansh she said, "Are you ready to go home?"

"What do you think? I've been living for the two of us to be alone."

"I'm glad you said that because I can't wait, either." She opened the front passenger door for him. He watched her press the tip of the handle, then pull it. He left the wheelchair and climbed into the front. Dr. Tullia shut the door. Luna thanked both men and went around to get behind the steering wheel.

She started the engine and they took off,

but he noticed she drove with restraint. "There are several cars following us at close range," he murmured.

"Security. You've been the Crown Prince and were assigned bodyguards. You'll get used to them."

Never.

"How do you like your car?" she asked. "If you want to drive, I'll pull over and change places with you."

"I'm glad you're at the wheel. It gives me a chance to look around." In truth, he loved looking at her.

"Would you like to take a tour of the city? Drive up around the royal palace?"

"I'd rather go home."

"Then that's exactly what we'll do. Viola has made lunch for us. If I know her, she's fixed your favorite pizza and homemade *pasticciotto*. It's a cream-filled pastry to die for."

"That's the goal. To put on weight." He turned to stare at her adorable profile. "*Grazie* for the clothes."

"*Prego*. That means *you're welcome*."

"*Prego...prego...prego...*" He said the word several times. "What am I wearing?"

"A dark blue *camicia* I love, *pantaloni* and *sandali* on your feet."

"Finally, some shoes." He repeated the words several times.

She flashed him another smile. "You're back in your world, Rini, even if you don't recognize it."

"You have no idea how good it feels to be free. But I need to be able to communicate. Can we work on my Italian today?"

"We're doing that right now. For as long as you like."

She'd taken a turn that led them up the lush hillside of the city. On the summit of one hill sat what he considered a small, peach-colored palace. Luna kept driving toward it and turned in to the driveway. They wound around the back next to two other cars. Beyond them he saw a garden of fruit trees. He blinked.

"This is *our palazzo*?"

She turned off the engine and grinned. "You look like I must have looked when you brought me here for the first time. It was built in the eighteenth century."

The fact that this had been his home was

surreal to him. "What does it have? Fifty rooms?"

"More like twenty in all. Viola and Mateo have their own apartment on the first floor."

"Where's our bedroom?"

"We have a suite on the second."

"I'd like to see it." He got out of the car and walked around to the rear to wait for her. She joined him and pressed on the remote. The lid opened. He pulled out the suitcase with his unbandaged arm and shut the lid. Suddenly, he heard voices and turned to see a middle-aged man and woman approach. Realizing who they were, he tried out his Italian on them. They teared up and bowed to him.

"Luna? Tell them I like doing things myself and will take my own suitcase upstairs."

She talked to them for a minute, then turned to him. "Let's go in and get settled. Viola will have lunch for us in the dining room whenever we're ready."

He followed her to the rear entrance that opened into an entrance hall. She explained that the kitchen area and laundry were down one hall to the left. He'd find the staff's apartment on the right.

She continued down a hall to the front of the *palazzo* with an ornate salon and sitting room. Paintings adorned the walls, mirrors, frescoed ceilings, chandeliers and parquet floors. But as they ascended the curving staircase, he much preferred looking at the feminine way his wife moved.

At the top of the stairs she turned right and opened the floor-to-ceiling paneled doors to their suite. It was another world, totally modern in decor with white walls, a living room with comfortable couches and a television set, a state-of-the-art business office with a large painting, and a bathroom.

He gravitated to the blue-and-yellow bedroom with a striped spread covering the king-size bed. Sunflowers had been arranged in a vase on the double dresser with some small framed photos. He noticed yellow lamps on the bedside tables. The windows had white shutters that let in the sunshine. How could he not have remembered any of this?

Her green eyes studied him. "What's the verdict?"

Rini liked it. "I can live in this suite." He lowered the suitcase to the tile and looked around, still incredulous that nothing produced a memory.

She broke into a glorious smile. "I'm glad to hear it since we had this part of the upstairs renovated and chose everything together. Whether you know it or not, you picked the blue-and-yellow scheme. I happen to love the combination, too."

Before he knew it, she put the suitcase on a nearby chair and opened it to take his things to the bathroom. Rini took advantage of the moment to remove his sandals and stretch out on the bed. When she emerged, she laughed. "You didn't need to worry. We made certain that oversize bed fit those powerful legs and big feet of yours."

"Join me and let's see how well it accommodates both of us."

Luna walked toward him. "I wanted to join you on the hospital bed in Rezana." After kicking off her sandals, she lay down next to him, turning to rest her head on his extended right arm.

She caressed the side of his jaw and pressed her lips to his. "You have no idea how long I've been waiting for this moment," she whispered in a breathless voice.

"I have my husband back and I'm never going to let you out of my sight again."

As her arms went around him, he brushed his lips over her cheeks and eyelids. He relished every part of her, exploring further until he'd covered every centimeter of her beautiful face.

"Rini—" she murmured, chasing his mouth with her own until she caught up to him. The second their mouths met, hers opened to him. He felt himself going under with a hunger that had been building.

Though he knew she was his legal wife, she was a stranger. Anxiety built up inside him. He felt like things were moving too fast with this woman he didn't remember who welcomed him so completely.

Somehow, he couldn't trust that she could be this loving with him when she knew he had no memory of her. Again, he feared that she pitied him and was trying to pretend all was well. Dr. Tullia had told him to discuss it with her. After a slight hesitation, he relinquished her mouth and rolled off the bed.

She sat up looking hurt. "I'm sorry, Rini. Did I do something wrong when I put my arms around you?"

He stood there rubbing the back of his neck in confusion. "You did nothing wrong. I've been wanting to kiss you, but…"

"But what?"

"There's a question I have to ask you."

"Go ahead. Anything."

His body grew taut. "Do you pity me? Because if that's the reason you were so loving with me just now, it's the last thing I want from you."

She moved to the side of the bed and stood up. He could hear her mind working. "I've been dying to crawl into your arms since the moment I saw you drugged at the hospital. You have no idea how much I've missed you since the quake.

"If I was loving with you just now, it's because I'm so wild with joy that you're alive! I never want to leave your arms. But I can see that you have to learn to trust me before we can have an intimate relationship."

"I *do* trust you."

"Outwardly," she came back. "However, it's clear that the closeness we shared as husband and wife is something that will have to come about naturally, over time. Let's let it rest for now. Why don't you freshen up and we'll go downstairs for lunch?"

He'd put his hand in his pocket and made a fist. "I've hurt you, haven't I?"

Her head lifted, causing her gilt hair to swish. "You're wrong, Rini. You were honest with me, and I'm grateful. If we don't have that, we don't have anything."

Everything she said made sense. "You're right. Luna? Will you do me a favor and ask my grandfather if we can visit him this afternoon?"

"Of course. He and your grandmother will be thrilled. I'll call him now."

Rini *had* hurt her, but he couldn't help it. Luna had gotten on that bed and had climbed into his arms without hesitation. Nothing could have shocked her more when he'd suddenly pulled away from her. Wanting to make love with him, pity had been the last thing on her mind. Dr. Tullia's advice went round in her head.

*Don't hold back. Continue to be yourself. In time you'll know if he feels nonreceptive or smothered.*

*That's what worries me. How will I know?*

*Is there any doubt in your mind that he'll tell you? Your husband is assertive and doesn't keep his thoughts to himself.*

Dr. Tullia had known what he was talking about.

After the bathroom door closed, Luna reached for her purse lying on a chair and phoned the palace. She asked to be put through to Antonia, who wept when she learned Rini wanted to visit. They arranged for three o'clock in their private sitting room.

When Rini joined her, he acted like nothing had happened. They went down to the dining room for lunch. Viola had outdone herself and her efforts paid off. Rini ate everything. At that point they went back out to the car and she drove them to the ochre-colored palace, another larger, eighteenth-century landmark. En route, she taught him a few more Italian words.

After parking in front, they walked inside past staff and went upstairs to the apartment on the second floor. His grandparents were waiting for them. He greeted them with his limited conversation.

"Oh, Rini," Antonia cried for happiness. "*Bravo.* You have no idea how wonderful it is to see you walk into our apartment. I know you don't know me, but can we hug you?"

Luna translated. His gaze darted to her before he said, *"Sì."*

First, his grandmother threw her arms around him, then Leonardo hugged his grandson. Their eyes filled with tears. They were led into the sitting room. Rini sat on a chair next to Luna. She eyed her grandparents-in-law. "On the drive over here Rini told me he wants to fly to Rezana by helicopter to thank the police officer who helped him and me. Could that be arranged for tomorrow?"

"We'll do anything for him."

Again, she translated his grandfather's response.

"Rini also wants to send a donation to Doctor Miakar at the hospital."

"I'll arrange it today."

She turned to Rini and repeated his grandfather's answer.

Rini tried out the new words he'd learned. *"Grazie mille, nonno mio."*

Leonardo got up and grasped Rini's hands. "God has brought you back to us."

"How do you feel about meeting the family?" his grandmother asked. "They're all anxious to see you again."

She felt Rini's hesitation. "Could we put that off for a little while?" he murmured to her. Luna translated.

"Of course. I'll suggest we wait on that decision until you've had your checkup with Doctor Romano in a week."

Rini nodded, looking relieved when she explained to them.

"Would you like to walk around the palace and grounds?" Antonia queried.

Luna told him what his grandmother had asked but knew his answer before he responded. "Maybe another time."

"Rini's tired," she explained to his grandparents. "We'll come again in a few days for another visit. In the meantime, let us know when the helicopter will be available." She hugged both of them. Rini had already stood up. He said goodbye and the two of them walked out of the palace.

"If it's all right with you, I'd like to drive."

Aha. "I was hoping you wanted to." Like Dr. Romano said, it was up to Rini. Excitement swept through her that he was ready to take charge. Luna reached into her purse for the remote, which she handed to him. He pressed the icon that unlocked the doors. After helping her in, he walked around and got in the driver's seat. But he had to adjust the seat to accommodate his long legs.

Rini was a quick study. He'd watched her drive and knew what to do. His memory loss didn't hamper his driving. Her husband had always driven fast and today was no exception. He took them on a long drive around the city, probably driving security crazy. She pointed out a few landmarks for him. It shouldn't have surprised her he knew where to go when he'd decided to head to their *palazzo* on the hillside.

After they pulled around the back, he turned off the engine and looked at her. "I've been wondering about the gift I could give Zigo. He's the reason I'm home now."

"Yes, he is. I'll never be able to thank him enough."

"What would you think if we drive this car to the gold mine tomorrow? I'd like to take a look at it. Then we'll head to Rezana and deliver it to him personally."

"You mean give him your car?"

"Why not? I earned it with my own money, right? It won't be a gift from the taxpayers."

"No." Her heart was bursting with love for him. "Little does he realize what his kindness did for you. Oh, Rini. He'll be speechless and won't believe it. I can promise you it'll be the only one in the town."

He nodded. "We could arrange for a helicopter to fly us home from there."

"Your grandfather will arrange it."

His eyes lit up. More and more Rini was acting and sounding like the man she'd fallen fathoms deep in love with.

When they entered the *palazzo*, Viola met them with a bottled protein shake. Luna explained to him what it was. "She thought you might be hungry again. Dinner will be at seven."

He nodded and thanked her. After he'd carried it upstairs, he drank the whole thing while Luna looked on. "That wasn't bad." He put the empty bottle in the wastebasket in their bedroom.

"You'll need the title to the car. It's in your inner sanctum."

He followed her while she pulled an envelope out of a file cabinet. "Thank goodness you've always been so organized. When you give this to Zigo, he'll sign it and that's all there is to it." As she lifted her eyes, the look of desire in his made her go weak.

After a quiet moment, "What would I do without you?"

She couldn't hold back brushing her lips against his. "You'll never have to find out." Then she walked back to their bedroom. He came more slowly. She could tell he was upset about something. "What is it?"

"Luna—I feel so hampered because I can't speak Italian, and I keep bothering you to teach me. It isn't fair to you."

"*Fair* doesn't come into it. I'd be hurt if you wouldn't accept my help, but I can only imagine your frustration. That's why I bought a surprise for you."

She saw him swallow hard. "Can I see it now?"

*My darling husband...* "I don't know." She gave him a sly smile. "Can you wait?"

"No."

Luna laughed. "I knew you couldn't."

"Am I that transparent?"

"In certain ways."

His features sobered. "You have the advantage of me."

She fought to stifle a moan. No matter how much she wanted the barrier between them to go away, it remained. She reached into her purse and handed him his new phone. He lifted his head.

"Come over here. I'll show you an app."

They walked over to the bed and sat down. "The app teaches you how to speak Italian. The woman speaks Romansh and takes you through different conversations. She reads aloud an index. As each subject lights up, you can press it and then repeat what she teaches you in Italian. When you wake up in the middle of the night tonight, you can turn it on and practice."

His dark, handsome head turned to her. "How do you know I wake up?"

"I've been with you from the moment I found you. The last two nights at the hospital you woke up around three and were restless. You'd get up and walk around before going back to bed. I'm sure you'd had bad dreams. I thought this would be a good way to help you."

"Did I call out or say anything?" There was alarm in his voice.

"No."

A bleak look came from his eyes. "I'm sorry. When I asked you to sleep by me, I didn't realize what I was asking."

She moved closer to kiss his jaw. "You don't remember, but three months after we were married, I contracted a strain of flu that put me in the hospital. You stayed with me day and night and nursed me for a week after I got home. After the love you showed me, I could never make that up to you. If you don't believe me, ask your grandparents. You missed a week and a half of work."

"Were you close to dying?"

"Rini—of course not!" She walked over and sat on the side of the bed. "Come on. Push it and let's listen."

He did her bidding. "If I'd had this in Rezana, I would have gotten out of there within a day."

Without thinking, she put her arm around his back. "It kills me to realize what you had to go through."

He put the phone on the side table and pulled her into his arms. "It awes me that you didn't give up on me. If you hadn't talked to the officer and come to the hospital…"

Rini fell back with her and buried his face in her neck. They clung to each other. This time he didn't pull away from her. She felt like they were communicating at last. More than that, they were communing.

His mouth found hers. "Thank you for this gift. I have a feeling it's going to save my life in the dark hours of the night."

"Don't forget I'll be there, too." She pressed her lips to his. They kissed slowly and sumptuously.

"Let's continue this while we're both on top of the bed, *pulcina mia*." Together they got up and lay down so their arms and legs tangled. Luna had wanted this for so long, she was in pain for him.

"Careful you don't hurt your wound."

"It's already healing."

But no sooner were the words out of his mouth than *her* cell phone rang.

"Don't answer it," he whispered against her lips.

"I have no intention." She kissed him hungrily, wanting to forget the world, but the phone rang again.

After a third time, Rini moaned. "Someone is anxious to talk to you."

"You're right. I'd better get it."

He kissed her one more time. "Come right back."

She hated to leave his arms as she eased away from him and rushed to retrieve her phone from her purse on the dresser. Then she hurried back to the bed and checked the caller ID. Rini stared up at her with those intense gray eyes.

"It's your grandfather calling. I'm sure it's about tomorrow's plans." Luna clicked on.

Actually, it was Antonia who conveyed the message that Carlo would fly there in the helicopter and arrange for a car for them. He would be there at two to meet them at the police station. Then the three of them would fly home together.

They hung up and she told Rini what they'd talked about. Then Viola phoned.

Luna thanked her and clicked off. "Our dinner is ready."

"Are you hungry?"

No. She wasn't. But she didn't want to tell him that for fear he would think she wanted to get back on the bed with him. Of course she did, but she didn't want to come across too eager. She'd made herself totally available to him because she loved him and she was his wife. Maybe he was attracted to her, but she was still an unknown to him and his heart wasn't involved yet.

"I'm hungry for anything Viola cooks. Come on. We'll make plans for tomorrow since we'll need to leave early."

She couldn't tell if it was the answer he'd wanted. Dr. Tullia had reminded her that Rini was assertive. If he didn't want to eat dinner, he could tell her he'd rather stay up here with her. As she started for the doorway, he didn't call her back or reach for her. She had her answer for now, but what would happen tonight when they went to bed? It would be their first night strictly alone as man and wife since the quake.

# CHAPTER SEVEN

RINI FOLLOWED LUNA out of the suite and down the stairs. He'd hoped she would have said she wasn't hungry, either. She had no idea how he'd longed for the two of them to spend the next twelve hours enjoying each other in ways he'd been imagining in his dreams.

Though he was convinced she didn't pity him, he'd been lying to himself to believe she was truly ready to make love. He couldn't bear the thought that she was play-acting in order to prove her love to the husband who'd lost his memory. Rini might look like the man she'd married, but in his gut he knew he was still a stranger to her.

She was a stranger to him, too. He had to admit he felt somewhat uncomfortable about making love to a woman he didn't know or recognize. Rini might not remember the man he was, but to take her to bed this fast didn't speak well for him as a decent human being. Not with *this* woman. Not with the devoted *wife* who'd saved him from death. She deserved all the respect he could give her while they got to know each other again.

By the time they began eating dinner, he'd made a decision. For the time being he'd let the intimacy of their marriage grow at its own pace. Instead, he'd concentrate on learning Italian and work out his future. They planned to leave for the mine at six-thirty in the morning and stop on the way for breakfast. Later, they'd drive on to Rezana.

After thanking Viola for a delicious dinner complete with two different desserts he'd apparently loved, he asked Luna to excuse him. He explained that he wanted to spend time on the computer. "I need to familiarize myself with the mine and the maps."

"That's a marvelous idea. And remember that when you come to bed, the app on your phone will help you work on your Italian conversation during the night."

"I haven't forgotten your gift, Luna. It's making all the difference."

Though he wanted to kiss her neck, he resisted the impulse and left the table to go upstairs. Luna had sounded so pleased with his plans; he knew he'd done the right thing.

If pressed, Rini had little doubt she'd do her wifely duty, but he wanted her to desire him the way she'd portrayed in that photo of them. The picture of two people madly in love never left his mind. He prayed that one day he and Luna would get there again.

Two hours later he crept into the bathroom for a shower and shave. Luna lay on her side asleep. He could tell she wore a nightgown. It pleased him that she hadn't put on her running clothes.

To his surprise he didn't wake up until he heard her in the shower. Rini took advantage of the time to get dressed in casual trousers and a polo shirt. He'd found a valise in his study to pack some maps and graphs he'd run off the printer. It also held the title to the car. He was set.

When she walked into the bedroom, she looked a vision in a short-sleeved print blouse and white pants. Luna's figure did wonders for anything she wore, and she smelled divine. The woman took his breath. *"Buongiorno, sposa mia. Sei bellissima."*

Her luscious mouth curved into a smile. *"E tu, Rini. Molto, molto bello."*

He knew what it meant. *"Grazie."*

"I'm serious. You look wonderful, and already so different from the man Carlo and I flew home to San Vitano. I can tell you've been studying your Italian. *Bravo, sposami.* I'm speechless over the way you're picking it up so fast. If you can speak this well already, the men at the mine won't believe you have amnesia. Neither will Zigo."

A chuckle escaped his lips. "I've memorized a few paragraphs here and there. We'll see their reaction. Are you ready? My things are packed, but I don't have any money."

"Don't worry. I've got plenty. Day after tomorrow we'll go shopping for everything that was taken from you and go to the bank." She looked out the window. "It's going to be another hot, lovely day. You usually wear sunglasses. If you want them, your favorite pair is in the top right drawer of the dresser."

"I didn't notice them."

"They're probably under one of your casual shirts."

Rini walked over and found them where she'd predicted. He put them on and turned to her.

She studied him in a way that said she liked what she saw. "In the sensational car you plan to give away, you'll look like the most dashing race car driver on earth. When you pull up to the police station wearing them, they won't believe you're the same man who was fading away in the hospital just a few days ago."

"All the credit goes to you, Luna. *Mi hai cambiato la vita*."

"That goes both ways, Rini. Just so you know, from the moment we met, you changed *my* life, too." The throb in her voice touched his heart. He couldn't doubt her memories of him. That was something to treasure.

"Let's go."

They left the *palazzo* through the rear entrance. Rini helped her into the passenger side of the car before putting the valise in the cargo space. After he got in and started the engine she said, "Last evening I asked Mateo to take the car to the service station for gas and a quick inspection. He assures me all is well."

Rini should have known his wife would be on top of everything. "I was going to suggest we do that before leaving the city. You're amazing."

She shook her head. "Thank you. I'll remember that when I start doing things that displease you."

One black brow lifted. "Is that possible?"

"Oh, yes. Just give it time. We're still in the honeymoon phase." She'd said it with a twinkle in her eye.

"Is that what you're calling it?"

*The honeymoon phase with no honeymoon.* That needed to end soon.

He drove around the *palazzo* to the street.

"Rini? Before we reach the autostrada entrance, would you mind heading for the palace?" It sat on a hillside, visible from the highway. "The Baldasseri Gold Mining office is in a building at the rear of the estate. I haven't been in touch with Fabio, who must wonder if I'm even alive. He's always there by seven."

Rini had been so concentrated on himself and their world, he'd forgotten she'd been living another life without him for close to two weeks. "How long have you been out of the office?"

"Since the day before you left for the mine. I'll only pop in for a moment. You don't need to go in with me."

His hands tightened on the steering wheel. "Would you rather I didn't?"

Her head jerked toward him, swishing her silky hair against her cheeks. "Rini—why in heaven would I care? I only said that because I know you're anxious to get to the mine and I don't want to hold you up. You and Fabio are friends. Once he sees you, he'll want to talk. Please forget I asked. I'll call him tomorrow. It isn't important."

Her reasonable response made him feel like an inconsiderate heel. She'd sacrificed every minute for him since she'd discovered him in the hospital in Rezana. "Of course it is. Otherwise, you wouldn't have asked."

He sped up to reach the palace and she guided him around to the neoclassic building located beyond the greenhouses. Rini's grandmother had wanted to take him on a tour of the estate. However, on that day he hadn't been in a frame of mind to appreciate much of anything except being with Luna. He felt that way about her more than ever.

Last night Rini had decided to let the intimate side of their marriage grow at its own pace. But looking at her now, the last thing he wanted was to wait. Everything about her stirred his senses. The desire for her was more real than ever.

Before he'd turned off the engine in the parking area dotted with a dozen cars, Luna opened the door and was ready to jump out. "I promise I'll only be a minute."

"Luna—take all the time you need." He needed to calm down. "We're in no hurry."

"As long as you're sure."

"I am."

She closed the door and hurried up the walkway to the main doors of the Baldasseri Gold Mining Company. Unable to sit there, Rini got out to work off his restlessness. He looked around, incredulous that all this had been his world until his head had been injured in the earthquake. This estate, the palace, the office building—none of it meant anything to him.

Anxiety started to build inside him, but the sight of Luna coming out the doors of the office brought him relief. She filled his eyes. His wife was incredibly beautiful. Then he saw a brown-haired man who cupped her elbow as they walked toward the car where Rini lounged.

They were both laughing, and the way the thirtyish, good-looking guy acted proprietorial with her caused Rini's muscles to clench. He straightened as Luna ran toward him. "Rini? This is your friend and manager, Fabio Machetto."

*"Buongiorno*, Fabio," he responded. *"Come va?"*

Fabio answered something back Rini couldn't understand and it frustrated the hell out of him. Luna rushed to translate. "Fabio said he's so thrilled to see you. He feels like he's dreaming."

In the next instant the guy hugged him before stepping back and talking to Luna again. Their conversation didn't last long, and she got in the car before Rini could come around to help her. Fabio shut her door and walked back to the office.

Rini climbed behind the wheel. He couldn't take off fast enough for the autostrada leading to the border. The GPS guided him without problem.

"I'm sorry Fabio came outside with me, Rini. I asked him not to, but he didn't listen." The tension inside the car could be cut with a knife. "I know he made you uncomfortable hugging you like that, but he didn't mean to."

"The hugging didn't bother me."

"Then what's wrong?"

He took a quick breath. "I realize he's the one who hired you. Did he ever date you?"

She didn't answer right away. Finally, "He asked me to go to dinner with him a week after I was hired, but I turned him down because I wasn't attracted to him. We've been friends, nothing more."

"I think it's possible he hasn't gotten the message yet."

Luna looked over at him. "What makes you say that?"

"Because I just watched a man come out the door who's in love with you."

"No, Rini. He's my boss, nothing more."

"You're not a man and didn't see what I saw. The poor devil. I realize it's nothing you can help."

"Rini, you're the only man in my life who ever made my heart come close to jumping out of my body. I'm so in love with you it's ridiculous!" She laughed, sounding too happy for words. "I can quit working. If you want to know the truth, I'd much rather stay home with you full-time and be your wife and Italian tutor. After almost losing you, I want to spend every living moment with you from now on. Say the word and I'll send in my resignation in the morning."

Rini shouldn't be so excited over her reaction. "You mean it?"

"Yes. When we were married, I didn't want to become a clingy wife, so I told you I preferred to keep working. But I didn't plan on doing it once we started a family."

"You won't miss going to your job every day?"

"There's a different kind of work being home with a husband who's having to learn a new language. I plan to be there every step of the way while you put your new world together piece by piece."

"Let's think it over, Luna. I don't want you to make a decision you'll regret." He'd talk to Dr. Tullia about it at his next session.

Luna rolled her enticing green eyes at him. "If anyone will regret it, it will be you, having to put up with a wife around the clock."

If she only knew...

Luna squeezed her eyelids shut for a moment. Had Rini been jealous? If it was true, it meant he was starting to care for her on an emotional level. She'd leave her job in a second knowing it was what he wanted.

But once again, he hadn't asked her to quit. Was that because *he* had to think it over? She'd promised herself she wouldn't push him. What would Dr. Tullia have to say about it? Maybe she'd call him and get his opinion.

Halfway to the mine they came to a village and enjoyed an al-fresco breakfast of *caffe al vetro* and large croissants that melted in your mouth. Rini ate four of them piled high with butter and plum preserves. At one point he reached out to flick some preserves at the corner of her luscious mouth into his. Little by little he was clearly finding it difficult to keep his hands off her.

Before they left the *trattoria*, Rini bought

a half dozen more croissants to take to Zigo. The tension between them had vanished and she was in heaven.

They drove on toward the border, passing lush greenery and forests. Rini looked at her as they neared the signs for the mine located at a higher elevation. "You've lost your smile. Are you all right?"

"Yes and no," she answered. "My emotions are bittersweet knowing that I got my husband back while seven of your former miners are buried here."

"I have no memory of them. But after waking up to find myself covered in debris, I'm as horrified as you are."

"Oh, Rini—" she cried out and gripped his arm. "I shouldn't have reminded you."

"I'm glad you did." He rubbed her hand before she let go. "I'll be meeting whoever is at the head of the mine in a minute. Everyone working there has lost a friend or coworker."

How she loved her husband! "They realize you were in the mine when the quake struck and will be overjoyed to see you alive and well."

"Stay with me when we go inside. I'm going to need you."

"Maybe now you know how I feel about you. I was barely alive after your grandparents came over with the news."

Rini slowed down as they turned down the road leading to the above-surface portion of the mine. "I brought some maps with me. This appears to be the entrance."

She undid the seat belt and leaned forward. "I've never been here. You promised me that one day you'd bring me."

Their gazes locked. "Who would have thought it would be under these circumstances?" After putting the sunglasses in his pant pocket, he got out of the car and walked around to help her. Once he'd retrieved his valise, they entered the modern-looking building. Luna never stopped praying that he'd see something that would bring back a memory.

Once inside she heard a man call out Rini's name. Suddenly, five people came running out of the office and engulfed him in bear hugs. He'd already had his christening with Fabio. She'd known he was loved and revered by people, but this show of affection had to warm his heart as it did hers.

One of the men turned to her. "Princess Baldasseri, I'm the acting head of the mine, Pesco Bonetti." He introduced the other men in turn. They all shook hands with her. "This is a great day." Their eyes had filled with tears. "Thank you for what you did for the miners' families. We won't forget."

"I did it for Rini," she said, wiping her own tears away. "I'm sure you've all heard my husband has lost his memory. He's working on his Italian, but for now I'll translate for him. We've come unannounced. If you don't mind, he'd like to meet with you for a few minutes."

"Come this way."

Luna looped her arm around Rini's and they followed the men into the office. Some chairs were pulled around and they met in a circle.

Rini opened his valise and pulled out the papers he'd brought. "Luna—ask Pesco to provide detailed information on the areas that I've checked and ask him to fax them back to me."

She handed the papers to the other man and explained what Rini wanted.

"I'd also like him to send me a review of the state of the mine since the quake. Everything he can think of to fill me in."

Luna continued to translate.

"Does this mean he's still in charge like before?" Pesco asked Luna in an aside.

"I don't know yet. We haven't discussed his future, but he feels a terrible responsibility even if he doesn't remember."

Pesco nodded. "Understood. I'll prepare everything and have it faxed to His Highness."

Rini turned to her. "One last thing. Thank him and all the men here at the mine for carrying on. I'd like him to send me any issues that haven't been resolved yet. The men of this mine have been the mainstay of the country and the monarchy. I'm here for them."

Struggling not to break down, she translated what Rini had said. After she'd finished, heads lowered and she heard sniffing. Pesco got to his feet and eyed her husband. "Tell him we're behind him all the way and welcome him back. This visit has renewed our faith."

Luna relayed this last message to him before they walked out of the mine to the car. Rini remained quiet. When she couldn't stand the silence any longer, she said, "You may not remember your past, but what you said and did today has won the hearts of those hardworking men.

"They'll never forget that the Crown Prince is a man just like they are. They know he's fair-minded and kind, that he's watching out for them and their families. You couldn't have sent a more important message. I'm so proud of you, I could burst."

"Please don't." His teasing voice brought laughter and tears. "What was it Pesco said to you at the beginning?"

"He thanked me for honoring the families of the miners who were killed."

"What did you do?"

"I met each family with flowers, and had the palace send them financial compensation for their loss."

His dark eyes pierced hers. "I'm the proud one that you would do that."

"I learned from you."

He reached for her hand and squeezed it. "You did exactly the right thing for them. Do you know you're the perfect wife?" In an unexpected move he leaned over to press an urgent kiss to her mouth. She never wanted him to stop.

In a minute he pulled away and put on his sunglasses. They were off, but she reflected on what he'd said. Luna didn't like being described as perfect, but knew it was meant as a compliment.

Before long the cluster of villages Rini had once described to her came into view on the horizon. Rezana was the first town located over the border, the one she'd seen from the air before the helicopter landed. By some miracle Rini had made his way out of the mine and had walked this far, looking for help.

What a shock it must have been to have fallen on the highway, let alone be taken to a hospital. He hadn't been able to communicate. The thought of it knotted her stomach.

They drove into the small town. She looked at the buildings until she saw police headquarters and the word *policija*. "There it is, Rini."

"I see it. Reminds me of *polizia* in Romansh."

"It's the same in Italian."

"I've got a lot to learn, don't I?"

"You've made remarkable progress already."

He pulled up in front.

"Does the front look familiar?"

"No. Neither did the mine. I had prepared a speech to say to the miners, but when the men ran over to hug me, I forgot everything."

"That was a sight I'll never forget."

Rini reached for her hand one more time and kissed it. "Thank you for being my savior." Again, she understood what he was trying to say, but she'd rather be thought of simply as his wife. "Shall we go in and hope to find Zigo?"

She got out before he could help her. Rini opened the cargo space to pull out his valise and the sack of croissants. Together they entered the police station. Luna rejoiced to see Zigo in the front office. He was alone. This was going to be fun!

"*Ciao*, Zigo," Rini called out to him, setting his valise on the floor.

The man looked up and got to his feet. His gaze swerved to Luna. "It's *you*!"

She nodded. "My *marito* has come to thank you for saving him."

Rini took off his sunglasses and approached Zigo, whose eyes almost popped out to see the change in him. *"Impossibile!"*

Her husband smiled and put the sack of croissants on the desk. *"Per te."*

"For you, Zigo," she said. "You were his salvation. He has another present for you out in front. Come with us."

Zigo appeared to be in a daze as he followed them out the front doors. Already a group of teenagers stood nearby, rhapsodizing over the car. In the distance she could hear the sound of rotors. Carlo would be landing any minute.

Luna smiled. "This is your car now."

Rini handed him the remote with the key. *"Grazie mille."*

"I don't understand."

"You helped my *marito*. He wants to thank you."

Zigo shook his head. "You give me this car?"

*"Sì."* Rini nodded.

*"Aie-yai-yai!"* Zigo's reaction was priceless. He held up his hands with his palms facing Rini. It was his way of saying he couldn't believe what was happening.

Thank goodness the helicopter landed at

the side of the station and Carlo emerged to join them. "I'm so glad you're here, Carlo. Rini is giving this car to Zigo for his help, but he doesn't think this is real. Will you explain to him in Slovene?"

She walked over to her husband while they waited for Carlo to talk to Zigo. In a minute the light dawned, and the officer hurried over to Rini. Carlo translated as the words came pouring out of Zigo.

"I never had anything given to me so wonderful. I don't deserve it."

Rini nodded. "Tell him when he helped my wife, he gave me my life back. I want to repay him with something I hope he will love. It's easy to drive and there's a booklet in the car."

Luna translated so Carlo could convey the message. Zigo's eyes filled with tears before he gave Rini a huge hug and broke down. She watched her husband hug him back.

"Carlo," Luna murmured. "Rini has the title and will sign it over to him with you as witness. We'll do it inside."

After the officer had recovered, the four of them entered the office. Rini pulled the title out of the valise and signed it over to

Zigo, who also signed and dated it. Then Carlo explained about the sack.

Zigo kept staring at Rini with tears in his eyes. Her husband's dramatic transformation had shocked him. Bit by bit her husband was acting more himself even though he remembered nothing.

But what if he never did recover his memory? She'd tried not to think about it, but that eventuality had to be faced.

Before they left, Luna had a last message for Zigo that Carlo translated. "You helped me when I thought all hope was gone. Bless you for your goodness."

Zigo smiled at her and told Carlo, who said, "Your eyes spoke to my soul when you talked about your husband. I wanted to help."

Luna reached out to hug Zigo. Rini followed with a strong handshake and picked up his valise. The three of them walked outside to the helicopter. Zigo accompanied them. While Rini helped her on board, Carlo chatted with Zigo for a few minutes, then came on board.

Luna could tell by the gleam in those gray eyes that her husband was pleased. She knew the second part of today's mission had now been accomplished.

For the short flight back to San Vitano, Rini kept his fingers tangled with hers, never letting go. There was only one problem. She wanted to feel more than his hand holding hers. Luna experienced pain that she couldn't appease her hunger for him.

She craved the physical closeness they'd once shared. She wanted to tell him about the baby, but that raised another disturbing question. Would he want to start a family now? So much had to be going on inside him. It was another point she needed to discuss with Dr. Tullia.

Today's visit to the mine where Rini had been caught in the quake had to have filled him with terrifying memories, yet he hadn't indicated he was disturbed. The visit with Zigo seemed to have made him happy.

Luna stared out the window at the velvety green landscape below. If only she could get inside his brain to know what was really going on.

His wife was being particularly quiet. Once again, Luna had asked nothing for herself and did whatever he wanted with a smile. His needs had reduced her to a caregiver who waited on him around the clock, and his guilt hung heavy. This evening he wanted to do something to thank her but would wait to talk to her about it until they returned to San Vitano.

The helicopter landed at the rear of the palace. After parting company with Carlo, a limo drove him and Luna to the *palazzo*. He noticed their bodyguards following them. It was something he would have to get used to.

Their driver wove around to the rear. Rini helped her out, relishing the excuse to hold her arm. Anything to be close to her. When they reached the *palazzo* back entrance, he paused.

"What do you think if we go in and get dressed up?" He'd seen a summer suit in his closet that would do. "I'd like to take you to dinner where we can eat and dance. I'm sure you know such a place, so I'll leave the choice up to you. Would you like to do that, or are you too tired?"

Her expression lit up. "You've been reading my mind."

*"Bene,"* he murmured with satisfaction.

On impulse he lowered his head to kiss that enticing mouth. The second they connected, she slid her hands up his chest and around his neck. Her action brought her body close to him and he deepened their kiss. "I've been wanting to do this all day."

*"Amore mio..."* she murmured, kissing him again with an ardor that set him on fire. At least this time he understood the words she spoke. That was progress.

*"Oh!"* a cry resounded. Viola had opened the doors. *"Scusa!"*

Luna broke away from him with a flushed face and said something to the housekeeper who nodded, then scurried off. In the next breath Luna turned to Rini. "I told her we're going out for dinner."

Much as he'd rather stay here and make love to her until morning, he'd promised her an evening out. "Let's go upstairs and get ready."

"While you shower, I'll phone to reserve a special table at Gilberto's."

He got the message and followed her up the stairs to their suite. "How special?"

"The one you arranged for us the night before we were married."

"Why is it so unique?"

"You'll find out." She flashed him an impish smile before heading into his study.

Rini rushed to shower and shave, excited at the thought of holding her in his arms while they danced. He pulled the pale blue suit from his closet and chose a darker blue shirt. As he was fastening it, Luna came into the bedroom.

"The bathroom is free, *mi biscottina.*"

She chuckled. "So now you're calling me a cookie?"

"Didn't I before?"

"No. Your Italian vocabulary has increased. *Bravo.*"

"Are we set for tonight?"

"We are."

He spun around. "Do I need a tie?"

"Not if you don't want to wear one."

"I don't."

"You look perfect to me." She disappeared into the bathroom.

# CHAPTER EIGHT

LUNA'S COMPLIMENT CAME so easily, but did she say that to him when in reality he probably should wear one? Because Rini was royal, was there a different standard of dress for him? Every time when things seemed to be going so well, he found himself second-guessing her responses. He needed Dr. Tullia's help. Tomorrow he'd ask Luna to phone the hospital and get Rini in to see him before the day was out.

He went into the study to put his valise away and work on his Italian to give her privacy. Before long he'd be able to call Dr. Tullia on his own and talk. That day couldn't come soon enough for him.

"Rini?"

He looked up and almost fell out of the chair. Tonight she wore a stunning black dress with spaghetti straps. The black high heels made her taller. She'd put on small diamond earrings that sparkled through her gilt hair.

*"Incantevole—"* He blurted another new word.

Her smile filled his universe. "What do you mean you don't speak Italian? For my husband to call me ravishing has made my day. I'm ready to go."

"We will in a minute. I can see I'm going to need a tie after all." He raced past her to get a silver striped tie out of the drawer and put it on. She waited for him at the top of the stairs. "Have you called for a limo?"

"No. We'll take our other car. It's the dark green sedan you saw parked in back next to Mateo's car. Here are the keys." She handed them to him, and they went down to the foyer.

Viola wished them good-night and they went out the back entrance to the car. Rini helped her into the car, loving the strawberry fragrance he now associated with her. Her skin looked like porcelain in the night light. It felt like velvet as he ran his hand down her arm before letting go, unable to stop himself.

Once ensconced in the elegant interior, Rini turned on the GPS to guide them to Gilberto's. Once they reached the street, he opened up and they took off.

She put a hand on his arm. "Just remember your bodyguards aren't race car drivers like you. Give them a little slack."

"Was I such a terror?"

"Yes."

"Finally, an honest answer!"

A delicate frown marred her brow. "What do you mean?"

Too late Rini realized his slip. "Forget what I said."

"I can't."

He took a deep breath. "Luna—you're always so wonderful to me and make me feel so good, I—"

"But you don't think I'm telling you the truth?" she broke in on him.

His wife sounded hurt. He groaned. "Yes, I do, but I know I couldn't have been a paragon to live with. Just now your comment seemed—"

"Real?" she cried out. "Does that mean you believe I've been lying to you from the beginning?"

"No. Of course not. It's just that I've had a hard time understanding how I married such a fantastic woman I couldn't possibly be worthy of."

"Worthy— Don't you think I have those same worries about you? At the hospital you woke up to find out you were married to a woman who means literally nothing to you. I've been shocked you wanted to come home with me. You could have asked Chispar to help you settle somewhere else."

"You're the only person I want to be with," he insisted.

"I'm thankful for that because I love you so much. But if the time comes and you want to move on and figure out your life without me, all you have to do is say so. I would never blame you if you wanted a divorce. You'd be free to do whatever you wanted."

He pulled onto a side street. Her words kept pouring out, crushing him.

"Rini? I've tried to imagine how ghastly it would be to wake up with amnesia and discover I was trapped in a marriage I didn't remember, with a stranger no less. Today you proved you can handle everything on your own."

He found a parking space and hit the brakes. "Except I need *you*, Luna!" A soft gasp escaped her lips. She stared at him with eyes full of tears. "I may have lost my memory, but I'm a man. Even before you told me you were my wife, I knew I needed the beautiful woman helping me with every fiber of my being."

She broke down sobbing quietly.

"Now is the time for total honesty, Luna. Do *you* want a divorce? Tell me the truth. We've got to have that, or we don't have anything."

Luna smoothed the hair out of her eyes. She cleared her throat. "Here's *my* truth. I want my life back with you, and I'm willing to do whatever it takes."

Rini reached out to squeeze her shoulder. "You took the words out of my mouth. I'm going to work on our marriage, and I have an idea. Let's pretend that we just met and want to get to know each other. On the flight home from Rezana earlier, I thought about how you've been waiting on me. I wanted to do something for you tonight to show you what you mean to me."

"Oh, Rini." She leaned over to kiss his

jaw. "I love it. A new beginning for both of us."

"Amen." He'd married an angel.

After kissing her mouth, Rini sat back and started the engine. He made a U-turn to get back on the autostrada and they took off until they came to Lago Diamanti. In the distance he saw a castle on the shoreline.

"You'll love this place," Luna murmured. "Part of the dining room extends out over the water."

His eyes took in the pines studding the landscape. "You're right. It looks like something right out of a storybook."

Incredible that he remembered none of this. Tonight he got the sick feeling that he'd never recover his memory. The blow to his head had wiped out that part of his brain. It appeared he'd spend the rest of his life working on a new life.

As for being a royal, he might have been born to royalty, but he wanted no part of it. Tonight he didn't want to think about it. Not when his exciting wife filled his vision.

"When you brought us here, I almost died it was so enchanting, Rini. The ripples on the water catch the light the way a diamond does. Long ago someone called it Diamond Lake and it stuck. The diamonds I'm wearing tonight are the ones you gave me that night for a wedding present."

"I'm starting to like myself better and better."

Her giggle made him smile.

A number of luxury cars filled the parking area. Rini found a space and shut off the engine. In the distance he heard dance music. The castle had been lit up like a Christmas tree. He helped Luna from the car, keeping his arm around her waist as they entered what looked like a thirteenth-century castle.

"Your Highness!" The host came running and greeted them, beaming from ear to ear. "It's an honor." He put his hand over his heart. "Come right this way."

Luna translated before following the man through a corridor to doors leading out to the patio. Couples were dancing to the music of the terrific band. Trees decorated with twinkling white lights gave the individual tables privacy. The host led them to the other end of the patio. Their table overlooked the water.

Once seated, he gave them menus, and a waiter took over. He poured them wine.

She looked at Rini across the small, candlelit table. Her eyes shimmered like green diamonds. "Do you trust me to order for you?"

"Why don't we eat the same meal we had when I brought you here before."

Luna gave the waiter the order before he left them alone.

"What are we having besides ham?" He drank some of the wine and liked it very much.

"You *knew* that word! As for the *pappardelle funghi*, it's a pasta with mushrooms."

He said the words, committing them to memory. Then he looked at her, needing to get her in his arms. "Signora Baldasseri, *ballerai con me*?" Rini had been practicing that phrase.

*"Mi piacerebbe."* She got out of her chair before he came around. That action told him what she'd said. Another word to put to memory. He caught her curvaceous body to his. She melted against him. "I can't believe I'm dancing with you again." Her voice caught. "It's a miracle that you're alive."

His lips roved over her soft cheek. *"You're* the miracle."

She nestled closer, clinging to him. "I'm in heaven, Signor Baldasseri."

He couldn't help running his hands up and down her back. "Luna—I want to make love to you when we get home. Is that asking too much of you? Don't be afraid to tell me the truth. If it's too soon…"

"Too soon?" She hugged him harder. "I'd hoped it would happen the first day I got you home from the hospital. But you held back because you thought I pitied you."

"I know that's not true now, but I need an answer to one more question. How badly do you want a baby knowing I've got amnesia? Does that change the idea for you?"

"Not at all. We're married and have decided to move forward. I want your child. Nothing would ever change that."

"So if I get you pregnant—"

"I'll shout from the rafters!" She stopped dancing and cupped his face in her hands. "Besides marrying you, Rini darling, I've wanted your baby more than anything else in this world. We've said we want to begin again, so the answer to both your questions is *yes!* I want to sleep with you in every sense of the word, and I can't wait for children. Whatever the future holds, we'll deal with it."

Rini let out the breath he'd been holding. "You've made me the happiest man on earth. I don't know if I can eat dinner."

"You *have* to, remember?" she teased. "Come on. Let's sit down so the waiter will serve us."

The next half hour passed in a blur. The food was sensational, but he couldn't take his eyes off Luna. "Do you want dessert?"

"I couldn't. What about you?"

Rini reached for her hand across the table. "I think you know the answer to that."

"I do." She put money from her purse on the table. "Let's go home." The pleading in her eyes was almost his undoing. He rushed around to help her, and they left the castle with indecent speed. On the drive back to the *palazzo*, he managed to elude a police car and his bodyguards.

She laughed as they pulled around the back. "All you have to do is present yourself as a race car driver and you can make your fortune in a whole new, exciting way."

"Well, there is this about it. At least if I crash during another earthquake, it will be above ground. Maybe I won't be able to speak Romansh anymore."

"Rini—you mustn't kid about things like that!"

He put a hand on her arm. "I agree that wasn't funny. Forgive me."

They got out of the car and went inside. She disappeared into the bathroom of their suite. He got ready for bed and threw on a robe while he waited for her. She emerged a few minutes later wearing a cream-colored nightgown.

"Rini? I should never have gotten so upset. The horror of believing I had lost you still lives inside me."

He shook his head. "I can't relate to your pain. What I do know is that if I lost you now, I wouldn't want to live."

The throb of Rini's deep voice resonated through Luna's body. She sucked in her breath. "You haven't lost me, and you never will." She flew into his arms.

*Adorata.*" Rini buried his face in her hair, then picked her up and carried her over to the bed. His eyes burned with desire as he lowered her to the mattress. "*Ti amo.* Do you hear me?"

Yes, she heard his avowal of love, but he didn't give her a chance to answer because his mouth had covered hers. This was the Rini she'd married over seven months ago, devouring her with the kind of hunger that aroused her deepest passion. He was alive and whole. She couldn't get enough of this beloved man who was her husband and had been returned to her.

With the robe and nightgown discarded, they lay there entangled while they tried over and over again throughout the night to assuage their need for each other. No man could be a better lover than Rini. She never wanted this rapture to end.

Toward morning she got her wish when he rolled her on top of him and made love to her all over again. Several hours later she cried, "I love you." She kissed every masculine feature of his handsome face. "I love you so much you can't possibly imagine. You've been so brave and courageous through all of this. I want to take away your every fear."

"You already do that by loving me."

"I want to do more. How can I help you?"

He propped some pillows and turned her in his arms. "I did a lot of thinking while we were at the mine. Obviously, it has been one of the mainstays of the family for three hundred years. Though I don't remember it, I believe it's still my responsibility.

"Since I have to do something with my life, I could choose anything. But it will mean I have to learn whatever it is from the bottom up and keep working on my Italian. So why not get involved in the administration aspect of the mine?"

She sat straight up. "That's a brilliant idea, darling."

"I could take a business class at the college along with a beginning Italian class. I'll discuss it with Doctor Tullia."

"Good. I have another idea."

"Of course, because you're my amazing wife." He gave her another kiss that swept her away.

"You could intern at the Baldasseri Gold Mining office several afternoons a week to get on top of the accounting. I could help you there, too. In no time you'll be in charge of the whole business you ran so beautifully for the country. I have no doubt of it."

The moment she said the words, Rini covered her mouth with his and once again he swept her away with unbridled passion. Her husband might have lost his memory, but he knew how to make her feel immortal.

Two hours later he lay on his side, drinking in her beauty. Because he didn't know she was pregnant and didn't remember what she'd looked like before, he didn't realize her body had changed. But in another month, he'd figure it out.

Right now she didn't want to worry about it and would have stayed here with him all day if her cell phone hadn't kept ringing until they couldn't ignore it.

Rini handed it to her from the bedside table. She answered, but because she was lying against him, she was in no state for a conversation with anyone. Dr. Tullia's secretary was calling to remind Rini of his appointment at eleven.

"He'll be there," she promised and hung up before kissing Rini. "You're due at the hospital at eleven for a session with Doctor Tullia. You're going to have to hurry to make it on time. Why don't you shower first while I ask Viola to get our breakfast ready?"

A sigh escaped his throat before he reluctantly moved away from her and reached for his robe. "Being in your arms has made me forget everything, *cara*."

He wasn't the only one with that problem. While he hurried to get ready, she called downstairs before phoning Antonia. "I know you're dying to see Rini again. I promise he'll talk to you before the day is out. I love you."

She passed Rini on her way to take a shower. He looped his arm around her shoulders to give her another kiss before releasing her.

Within a half hour they'd eaten and had hurried out to the car. Rini drove them to the hospital. Being independent made him more like the husband he'd been before the quake. She encouraged him to do as much as he could by himself.

After he turned off the engine, she put a hand on his arm. "I'm sure Chispar will be there, so I'll wait for you here."

"One day soon I won't need a translator. After I'm through, let's go to lunch and then stop by the office. You can orient me." Another quick kiss and he got out of the car. He'd worn a tan summer suit and white shirt with no tie. No man on earth looked as handsome as he did. Already she could tell he was putting on weight even though it hadn't been that long since his rescue.

She phoned Fabio and told him she was bringing Rini into the office later so he could familiarize himself with the accounts. Luna didn't have to get permission. Rini was in charge of everything and always had been. But she didn't want to surprise Fabio.

"How will he do that when he can't understand?"

"He's working on his Italian constantly. You'd be surprised how well he's progressing. See you later."

A half hour later Rini returned to the car, looking relieved. She flashed him a smile. "I can tell that session went well."

He started the engine. "I had a short conversation with him in Italian. It surprised him. When I told him of my plans, he said taking an English class online was fine, but no college yet. He says I need more time to work on my marriage to you. A trip to the business office might not hurt, but don't get overwhelmed."

"That's excellent advice. I'm sure he can't believe you're in such good spirits."

Rini drove out to the street. "I gave you all the credit for my rehabilitation. But my guess is he already figured that out the first time he met you. Besides being a stunning beauty, there's no woman to measure up to you."

"You spoil me with compliments like that." After a night of being loved by him, there was nothing wrong in her world. *Until* she remembered this was a new relationship to him. Maybe he was falling for her. But how long would that infatuation last? Could it survive while he tried to rebuild his life?

Luna was getting ahead of herself and needed to slow down. Take one step at a time and be thankful.

"That's quite a conversation you're having with yourself, *sposa mia*."

Warmth crept up her neck into her cheeks. "I've been thinking about the great strides you've made since a week ago. You're so courageous, I'm in awe."

"There you go again. Building me up so I feel I could accomplish anything."

She studied his chiseled profile. "You already have by staying alive until you were found. A lesser man would never have made it. You walked to the highway after crawling out of the mine. I don't know how you did it."

Luna's words found their way deep into his soul. Last night she'd taught him what it was like to be married to the most wonderful, giving, passionate woman on earth. Rini didn't deserve her. Not yet. But he'd do whatever it took to win her love again.

After leaving the hospital, they drove to the office. He parked in a reserved space near the entrance. Luna had told him there were eighty staff members who filled the two-story building. They dealt with the various departments. The accounting department contained three offices including hers on the main floor. Fabio had his own private office nearby.

Rini helped Luna out of the car and kept his arm around her waist as they entered the building. They passed a glassed-in office where an attractive young woman waved to them.

Luna waved back. "That's Suzanne. She and I have become good friends."

Within seconds they were ensconced in Luna's office. She put another chair next to hers in front of her desk so they could sit together. He looked around, noticing she had a wedding picture of the two of them on one wall. They'd just come out of the cathedral where she'd said they'd been married.

"That was the happiest day of my life," she murmured after noticing where his gaze had settled. "The only happier day was when I walked into that hospital room and saw you lying on the gurney."

He gave her a piercing glance. "As I told you before, I heard an angel's voice speaking to me. I couldn't believe it and opened my eyes to see this exquisite woman at my side. She'd just told me she loved me in a language I understood. I'll never forget that moment. I thought I was hallucinating when you said you were my wife. It didn't seem possible I could be married to you."

*"Rini..."*

Unable to suppress his desire for her, he

reached over to cup her face. Hungry for his wife, he started kissing her.

*"Mi scusi."*

A male voice broke in on them. Rini slowly relinquished her lips and turned. The manager stood in the doorway.

Rini got to his feet. *"No c'e problema. Ciao, Fabio. Come va?"*

His expression registered utter disbelief that Rini was speaking Italian. *"Bene, Rini. E tu?"*

*"Molto, molto bene."* He darted Luna a smile. *"Sto lavorando con mi bella moglie."* Rini said the words to make it clear to Fabio that he was back from the dead. Not only was he working with his wife, he was also more in love with her than ever.

Fabio's eyes swerved to Luna, staring at her. After a minute he left and shut the door behind him. Rini sat down again and hugged his wife. "How did I do?"

She leaned into him. "You already know the answer to that. Your transformation surprised the daylights out of Fabio."

"Did you tell him I would be coming to the office with you?"

"Yes. I phoned him while you were in session with Doctor Tullia. You'll always be in charge of this office and the mine, but I wanted to give him the courtesy of a heads-up this one time."

There was nothing about Luna he didn't admire. "You're a wonder."

"I hope you feel the same way after we've spent a few hours together on the books."

"I love being with you no matter what we do."

Her eyes gave off green sparks. "That sounds perfect. Are you ready to plunge in?"

"Ready and eager. Let's see what kind of a teacher you make."

"Oh, dear. I wish you hadn't said that."

He chuckled as she pulled up a file and they got started. Since numbers didn't have to be translated, Rini was able to grasp quite a bit for a first round. He hadn't lost his math capabilities. Luna made it easy by compiling a list of headings in Romansh. In another day or two he'd have the terms memorized into Italian.

An hour later they left the building to eat lunch. "What are you in the mood for, Rini?"

"I think fish."

"Then I know a perfect spot." They got into the car and she showed him where to drive to a port on the lake. "It's the place we love after we've been out swimming and fishing."

"On what?"

"You have a cabin cruiser."

"I do?"

"We've spent many a night on it."

Soon, they reached the port and she pointed out his sleek blue-and-white cruiser moored at the pier alongside half a dozen others.

"I've got an idea, Luna. We could move to the cruiser."

She laughed. "You used to say that to me whenever we'd been out on it. You loved being on the water."

"I'd like to see it. Why don't we pick up some lunch and eat it on board?"

"Let's do it, but I don't have the key for us to take a drive."

"I don't care about that."

It didn't take long for them to buy crab and pasta to go. The delightful news that they had a cruiser had excited him. She waved to the security guard at the dock, who recognized them. Rini helped her get on board and they went below deck out of the hot sun to eat. They sat together on the couch while they ate.

"Let's come out here tonight."

"I'd love it, but maybe we should wait until tomorrow."

"Why?"

"First of all, we need to go shopping so you'll feel like you've joined the world. You need a watch and wallet. And I think a few new casual shirts, too. And then this evening your grandparents are hoping to hear from you. We could run by the palace."

"I'd rather not."

"Then we'll set up a video conversation with them at the *palazzo*."

"I'm not ready to spend time with my grandparents yet."

"Why is that?"

He let out a sigh. "I had a long conversation with Vincenzo and ran it by Doctor Tullia. Vincenzo is being groomed to take over the monarchy when the time comes. I refuse to interfere with that. The earthquake changed everything. I have no desire to take on former duties I know nothing about. I don't want to do them, but I hate disappointing my grandparents.

"I realize they have expectations of me I can't fulfill. That's why it's hard to be around them. Can you understand that when it's clear my amnesia is here to stay?"

"Yes. I *can* understand. But you need to tell your grandparents the truth of your feelings."

"Doctor Tullia said the same thing. So tonight we'll call them and I'll explain what's going on with me. That's the best I can do."

"That's all anyone could ask."

"While we're on the subject, I've been thinking I could video call with the general manager at the mine."

"You used to do it with the various managers when you had to be away from the mine on your princely duties," she informed him.

"Good. With your help I can discuss the fax he sent."

"After a couple of months, you'll be able to handle everything on your own."

"As long as I'm with you. I need you in my life, Luna. You'll never know how much," he whispered, covering her lovely face with kisses. His appetite for her had become insatiable.

"Right now all I want to do is get you in my arms. He stood up and pulled her to him. Within seconds they reached the cabin and fell on the bed, feverish for each other. They ended up getting home in time to call his grandparents, but the shopping had to be put off for another day.

# CHAPTER NINE

"Rini?"

They'd just gotten off their online meeting with his grandparents. It had been a painful experience.

He shut down his laptop and shot to his feet. "I've done it now."

"You had to do it, *tesoro mio*."

"I may not know them, but I felt their pain."

Luna had felt it, too. She got up from the chair and threw her arms around him. She rested her head against his shoulder. "They're doing their best to understand. Give them time. Don't forget. Vincenzo is already there, ready to take over when the time comes."

He threw his head back. "I'm a monster, aren't I?"

"No, *amore*. You came out of that mine

a different person. It's been in God's hands and they know it. Come to bed."

That night they held each other and clung. Her beloved husband had been carrying a terrible burden. Thankful he'd made the necessary phone call, now maybe he'd finally get some peace.

The next morning she found him in his study on a call with the manager at the mine. The two managed to communicate with Rini's very modest grasp of Italian. Her pride in him was off the charts.

When the call ended, he turned and saw her. "You're awake. I didn't realize. During the night I got the idea to go down into the belly of the mine where the cave-in occurred. I know they've tried to remove debris, but I want to try it again to see if we can find some bodies. I despise feeling helpless. Maybe it's a fool's errand, but I have to try."

"No, Rini. I don't want you to go down inside."

"I'll be fine, but knowing how you feel, you won't be coming with me."

"You can't go!" she cried. "I won't let you."

He grinned. "I can see we're having our first fight."

"This isn't funny."

She heard him draw in a deep breath. "I knew you wouldn't like it, but it's something I *have* to do."

"Why?"

"I may have given up the idea of being Crown Prince, but a Baldasseri has been in charge of the mine for three hundred years. Now it's my turn. I'm responsible for the entire operation. The men look to me for direction. What kind of a leader would I be if I let my problems defeat me? I need to do everything possible."

She struggled to keep back the tears. "But all of that has been done."

He stared hard at her. "Did you give up on me?"

Rini had made his point. "I understand, but I have a horrible feeling about it."

"That's your fear taking over."

Yes. She *was* afraid. For him, for them, for their baby. If there was another quake or a cave-in, their son or daughter would never know him.

"Luna—I *must* do this." She heard his determination. His vibrant voice resonated to her insides.

She could tell him the truth now, that they were expecting a child. The knowledge would probably force him to accede to her wishes. But that would be a cruel thing to do to him when he'd just made his first big, courageous decision to stand at the helm.

"I know you do," she said at last, defeated by his excitement and that feeling inside him. "I'm sorry I had such a strong reaction."

"Forgive me for upsetting you, Luna, but nothing's going to happen to me. I'll be home by the end of the day."

Those were the very words he'd said to her before he'd left their bed to inspect the mine. To go through that horrifying experience again would be the end of her, but she couldn't think that way.

"Of course you will, and I'll be waiting."

She wanted her husband whole and healthy in mind and body. He'd been born with this drive. Rini needed to act on it in order to thrive.

He may have lost his memory, but he hadn't changed in the most fundamental way. Few men were natural-born leaders. His name had been preordained to be on a very short list. From an early age, he'd been revered. Now he was loved and respected by his country. This was his destiny.

Another quake could hit in the same region at the same intensity. But she couldn't live in fear of that or she'd never get through life. To hold him back for her own selfish reasons would be wrong and unworthy of her.

"We'll have today and tonight on the cruiser," Rini reminded her.

"I can't wait."

They got busy and left for the port, taking food with them from the *palazzo*. After they arrived, Rini started up the engine and they took off for a fantastic day of fishing and sunbathing. By that evening they'd stuffed themselves with food and went to bed.

Rini rolled her on top of him. "We'll make the most of this night. Tomorrow morning we'll drive to the palace and I'll take off for the mine in the helicopter. I promise I'll be home by six for dinner." Once again, they began the age-old ritual that brought both of them rapture. No woman ever had a husband as wonderful as Rini.

The next afternoon, as Rini walked through the claustrophobic labyrinths of the mine, the full realization of what had happened to him during the quake hit him. For the next few hours he and Pesco and the staff explored the area where the miners had been buried. It was an incredible sight to see all those boulders that filled the chutes. He lost total track of time because he was so deep in thought.

The massive damage was testament to the power of that quake. How he'd escaped death was absolutely astounding to him.

He'd studied the maps and found the shaft that led to the exit where he'd crawled out. Rini followed it and looked up at the sky. Maybe if he stood here long enough, a miracle would happen, and another quake would restore him to his former self.

He waited, but by eight o'clock he felt no tremors or rumblings. The ground remained solid beneath his feet.

"Rini?" Pesco murmured. "The men have gone home. Shall we go, too?"

He nodded and followed Pesco up to the

surface of the mine. Of course the men had left after such a disastrous meeting! Rini could never blame them. He wasn't the person he'd been pretending to be, and they knew it.

It would take him a lifetime to relearn what had taken him twenty-nine years to accomplish. There was no point in prolonging this nightmare. Not only couldn't he speak fluent Italian, he also didn't know what in the hell to communicate to the men. He knew nothing about running the mining world.

The only reason the men had treated him with the greatest deference was because they saw him as the Crown Prince, whatever that was. But Rini had seen the sadness in their eyes while he'd struggled to find words and come up with ideas that meant nothing!

They'd sent each other nonverbal messages when they'd thought he wasn't looking. But Rini had known what they were thinking. What was this shell of a man doing in their mine when it was the last place he was wanted or needed? He thought he could just walk in like nothing had changed because he was the grandson of the King? Who did he imagine he was kidding?

After thanking Pesco, he walked to the helicopter and told the pilot to head back to Asteria. His wife would be waiting for him.

Luna looked up and closed the book she'd been reading. "That's a morose expression on your face, *mi amante*. I have to admit I was disappointed to receive your text late in the afternoon. Thank heaven you're home safely. I worried something might have happened to you."

"Something *did* happen," he muttered. "Before I say anything else, I need a shower."

*"Rini—"*

The terror in Luna's voice didn't stop him. Rini tore off his clothes and got under the water. Ever since he'd been flown back to Asteria, he'd wished he could wash away this creature he'd become. Last night in talking to his grandparents, he'd felt depression descend because he couldn't remember anything about his former life.

Now he had to face the woman who'd been responsible for keeping him alive body and soul. He couldn't comprehend that a feat of that magnitude had even been possible.

He stayed under the spray until the hot water turned tepid. It wasn't until he realized nothing but cold water poured down that Rini shut off the taps and reached for his robe. Forget shaving. That could wait for another time. The talk with his wife couldn't.

Close to midnight, he entered the bedroom. Luna sat on the side of the bed in her robe, waiting for him. Her gilt-blond beauty with those beguiling green eyes never failed to stun him. She smiled. "The hot water must have run out long ago. If you hadn't made an appearance in another minute, I planned to come in after you."

Rini moved closer, needing to steel himself for what had to be said. "It was insensitive of me to stay in there so long. To compound my sins, not only was I late getting home and that frightened you, I also left you with unanswered questions. You would never do that to me."

She shook her head. "Rini—what's going on inside you? You're being positively mysterious."

He cocked his head. "Maybe that's because I *am* a man of mystery."

"An exciting one." The chuckle he loved escaped her lips, making this moment that much harder for him. Before long she wouldn't be chuckling.

Over the past few days, he'd tried to adopt Dr. Tullia's rule after being in a few sessions with him.

*Don't impose on her what you believe are her assumptions about you. Be honest with her. Let her tell you her honesty.*

But he couldn't follow the doctor's advice to be patient any longer. It was time to express his feelings that were ready to burst.

His heart thudded. "There's only one way for me to say this. I want a divorce."

She didn't move a muscle. Only shock could have caused the color to drain out of her complexion. But he'd started this, and now he had to go on even though it was killing him.

"There was a moment in the mine when I wished there'd been another quake." A small gasp escaped her throat. "If miracles were being handed out, I would get hit in the head again and awaken the same man I'd once been."

"Don't even think it!" she cried.

"You're not in my skin, Luna."

Another muffled sound came from her. A

shudder shook her beautiful body. "I don't know how you dared venture inside."

"You know why."

"Darling," she whispered.

"I didn't belong down there, Luna, and have no wish to put those men through that agony again. Or *you*."

She clasped her hands. "You think I'm in agony?"

"I *know* you are," he bit out. "You think I didn't understand what went through your mind when you learned I'd completely lost my memory? We were both strangers to each other. I'll never live up to your expectation of who I used to be. I don't want to try. I'm exhausted trying to reinvent myself. It's not working."

Spots of color stained her cheeks. "You don't know what you're saying."

"Oh, yes, I do. Like I told Doctor Tullia, you're an angel. Too perfect. You never make a misstep. When we vowed to love each other for better or worse, we didn't know I would turn into the amnesiac I've become. You deserve to start over again with someone who will fall in love with you."

"Because you're *not* in love with me?" she fired at him.

"I'm not worthy of you, Luna. You need to be free. Since the moment I woke up in the hospital in Rezana, I've clung to you. My total selfishness has made your life a living hell."

"Stop, Rini! Don't you know how thrilled I've been that you've wanted me with you every second? After all, I'm a stranger to you."

"But you can't leave a room without my questioning it. Every second I'm awake, I need you. When I'm asleep, I need you right by me. No move has been made without my devoted caregiver right there at my side."

"There's no other place I want to be."

"Spoken like a dutiful wife."

"Not dutiful. I love you. If I didn't, I would have told you I wanted a separation before we ever left the hospital."

"Because of your selflessness, you've brought me through the worst of my reincarnation. But from now on I'll be able to survive on my own. The whole point is that you must be released from the bondage of our marriage to be the person you were meant to be. I've become too possessive of you. It's not right. You're only twenty-six with a lifetime ahead of you. To be chained to me would rob you of your destiny."

She got to her feet. "Where has all this come from? What have you been holding back I know nothing about? Tell me!"

"Vincenzo mentioned that he'd come to the rescue because you needed space and my grandparents were worried about you having to be there twenty-four-seven."

Luna shook her head. "You mean to tell me that what Vincenzo said has caused all this doubt and fear in you?"

"Can you deny you feel chained to me?"

"I deny it a million percent!"

"No, you don't, but you're too committed to me to say anything else. This isn't the life either of us signed up for. I can't live with the guilt of depriving you of your expectations. You say we met and fell madly in love. I accept that we did. But I came out of that mine a different man.

"You should be able to meet another man and fall in love with the knowledge that he'll always be that same man. The two of you can build a life together and realize your dreams."

She clasped her arms to her waist. "What about yours?"

"I don't have any, Luna. I'm still trying to survive. My grandparents are waiting for some transformation that isn't going to happen. As for my position at the Baldasseri Mine, I'm giving it up."

"How will you live?"

"I do have the savings in my account that I've earned. It's enough money to get me started in a new direction. More important, I'll make certain that you will always be taken care of and retain your title. This *palazzo* and everything in it is yours for your lifetime. You will want for nothing."

"Except for the man I love." The tremor in her voice could have been his undoing if his mind wasn't already made up.

"Face it, Luna. He died in the quake."

"Have you talked to Doctor Tullia about this?" She sounded frantic.

"I don't need to. He can't change me into the man I once was. No power on earth is capable of that."

She stood in front of him, her eyes burning like green fire. "So there's nothing I can say?"

"No. For better or worse doesn't apply to us. I'm not the man who made that vow to you. I could never live up to the person you married. I'm not the man you chose to be your husband. It isn't possible."

Luna put a hand on his arm. "I want the man I'm looking at right now, flaws and all."

Rini stepped away. "But I don't want you, not under these circumstances."

Moisture glistened on her eyelids. "Can't you pretend we've just met and start all over again, like we decided at the lake?"

He shook his head. "We'd be living a lie for the rest of our lives. It's not going to work for either of us."

Tears ran down her cheeks. "So you're going to end everything, just like that? Rini—" She staggered to the nearest chair and sat down.

He couldn't take much more of this and headed for the door of their suite. "On the flight home from the mine I worked out a plan. Tonight I'll sleep in the guest room down the hall. Tomorrow I'll go to a hotel."

"And then what?"

"In the morning I plan to buy a car. By afternoon I'll meet with an attorney to expedite the divorce. Don't worry about anything. My grandparents are kind people who've given me the breathing room I've needed. I couldn't ask for better. They love you and will supply you with the best counsel available."

He opened the door. "With that said, I'll say good-night. As of now, you're free to embrace the life you were meant to live. In case you didn't know it before, I'll tell you now. You *are* the best."

Through blurry eyes Luna watched her husband leave. He'd delivered his ultimatum. She'd known no power under heaven would cause him to change his mind. If she'd told him they were going to have a baby, that would have hastened his exit from the room. His guilt over divorcing her would increase. The last thing she wanted to do was overwhelm him. The revelation they were expecting would have to come later when she could think.

An hour passed while she toyed with the one what-if idea she'd been entertaining in her mind. He'd thrown down the gauntlet, but unlike the knights of old, he didn't expect her to pick it up.

Luna had news for him.

Considering she had nothing to lose, she got to her feet and started for the entrance, determined like she'd never before been in her life.

"Rini?" She knocked on the guest bedroom door.

"Come in," sounded his deep voice.

Surprised it was that easy to gain access to his new inner sanctum, Luna entered the room. He'd propped himself on top of the bed with his laptop. Those long, powerful legs were visible below the hem of his robe. "If you're here to argue with me, it would be useless." She noticed his gaze never left the screen. He'd gone into battle mode.

"I know that. I came for a different reason."

"What would that be?"

She sat down on the end of the bed, close enough to touch him, but she resisted the temptation. "Before you put your plans into motion tomorrow, I'd like to ask a favor of you."

That request captured his attention. His dark head lifted, and their eyes met. Rini's male beauty had never been more evident. "Go on."

"Since you've been home from Slovenia, it dawned on me we haven't taken a trip or been anywhere together. There's been no time for us to relax and just have fun. Between everything, we haven't had the opportunity to simply enjoy ourselves."

He closed his laptop. "I wasn't aware you wanted to get away. Why didn't you say something sooner?"

"We've been so busy I haven't even thought about taking a break from routine. But since you've decided you want a divorce I'm hoping you'll take me on a vacation before we go our separate ways."

"You can leave anytime."

"I wouldn't want to travel alone. That wouldn't be any fun at all."

One black brow lifted. "You never mentioned wanting to go on a trip."

"Where would I go? Why would I want to do anything without you?"

"You could have asked your friend Suzanne at the office."

"No, Rini. I was too grief stricken to make any plans. But all that changed after Zigo helped me find you and bring you home. Since we've built a friendship over the time you've been here, I think we could have a terrific time together. Why not celebrate your freedom? We'll speak Romansh to our heart's content and forget Italian. When we get back to San Vitano, you can visit with your grandparents and tell them your future plans."

She could hear his mind working. It was a good sign he hadn't shut her down yet. Her heart leaped when he said, "If I were to agree, do you have a destination in mind?"

"Yes! I'd love it if we took a driving trip down through Bolzano and Venice. We could visit some wonderful little out-of-the-way spots and walk around without worrying about a schedule. I was thinking a week maybe. Does any of that appeal to you?" They'd gone to Venice on their honeymoon. This was a last-chance effort to see if anything triggered his memory.

Though he said nothing, at least he hadn't given her an outright no yet.

"Why don't you think about it, Rini? Tell

me in the morning at breakfast. Remember it's only an idea. I promise I won't fall apart if the answer is no."

Not wanting to overstay her tenuous welcome, she got off the bed and headed for the door. It delighted her that silence followed her into the hall and back down to their suite.

Dr. Tullia had told Rini he could call him anytime, even the middle of the night. After being unable to sleep, he took him at his word and phoned him at home at six in the morning. Somehow, he'd try to make himself understood despite his difficulty with Italian.

"Rini—what a surprise!"

"Sorry, but I need help."

"Talk to me."

"I divorce Luna. She wants vacation first. I don't."

"Why not?"

Frustrated by the question, Rini jumped out of bed and began pacing. "I want divorce now."

"She found you?"

He blinked. *"Sì."*

"She made you happy?"

"*Sì.*"

"Then no problem. Your turn to make her happy now. *Correto*?"

Rini heard the words loud and clear. "*Correto.*" Good old Dr. Tullia knew what he was doing all right. The woman hadn't asked anything of him until now.

Bowing to the older man's wisdom, Rini said, "*Grazie, Dottore.*"

"You're welcome. Call me anytime."

He hung up, standing there in a daze. As Rini thought over the time they'd been together since the quake, and all that Luna had done for him, shame consumed him. After breaking his promise to her yesterday, he'd come home late from the mine last night. With no lead up at all, he'd blurted that he wanted a divorce. To make certain she understood, he'd announced he'd be sleeping in the guest bedroom until he moved to a hotel.

But he *would* agree to take her on a trip.

With his mind made up, he went down the hall to their bedroom. He could hear the shower running. Now would be the best time to get dressed in casual clothes and meet her in the dining room.

Once he was ready, he grabbed his wallet and hurried downstairs. Viola greeted him with a cheery voice. She poured hot coffee for him and Luna and put a plate of freshly baked rolls on the table.

Rini enjoyed the homemade plum jam he'd learned came from their fruit trees out in back. He piled it on with butter. When Luna entered the dining room looking ravishing in a yellow print sundress, he'd eaten three rolls.

Her green eyes widened in surprise to see him. "*Buongiorno*, Rini."

He got up and pulled out a chair for her. As usual her flowery fragrance assailed him. "I thought we were going to speak Romansh from now on."

She lifted her head. "Does that mean what I think it means?" The happiness in her voice told him all he needed to know.

"I'm ready to leave on that trip whenever you are."

Viola appeared with plates of eggs and ham. Rini dug in. Luna barely touched her food. He'd put her lack of appetite down to shock that he'd capitulated. She told the housekeeper they were leaving on vacation and would be gone a week.

"I'm so happy for you." Viola beamed.

"So am I. All we have done is work, work, work. It's time to play."

She put her hands on her ample hips. "That's exactly what you should do! Mateo will get the car ready for you."

"Thank you, but we won't be taking the car, Viola."

"You're going to fly?"

"No." Luna looked at Rini. "We're going to buy another car."

"Ah. To replace the car you gave away." With that response, Viola left them alone.

"Why would we want a different car?" She'd aroused Rini's curiosity.

"We're going to travel incognito. Everyone stares at us when we're out in public. 'There's the Crown Prince!' people cry out. I want us to be unrecognizable, like a typical couple enjoying the day. We can pick up the car I have in mind on our way out of Asteria. It's commensurate with our income."

He grinned, loving her creative mind. "How much do I make?"

"We work in a laundry and barely bring in enough to afford a seven-day trip, let alone a vehicle to get us where we want to go. I'll call your grandparents and tell them we're leaving. I'll also let Fabio know I won't be in for another week. Finish your breakfast while I hurry upstairs to change and pack. We'll only need one medium-size suitcase."

Again, she'd piqued his interest. "How come?"

"The car we're buying will only hold one. All we'll need are shorts, T-shirts, sandals and hats. We'll throw in a swimsuit. That's it!" On that note she disappeared from the room.

# CHAPTER TEN

RINI WAS STARTING to get excited.

Once he'd finished eating, he hurried upstairs. *"Ehi!"* he burst out after opening the door.

At first, he thought another woman had invaded their bedroom. His attention was caught by the blue tie-up sandals on a pair of gorgeous legs. It took a moment to realize Luna had changed into pale blue shorts and the craziest T-shirt he'd ever seen of a fat marshmallow whose hair was on fire.

Most amazing of all, she'd swept her blond hair on top of her head. It was hidden by a baseball cap she wore backward. Green sunglasses completed the picture of a wacky woman with the most sensational figure he'd ever seen on a woman.

"Think I look like Princess Baldasseri now?"

He shook his head. "Your transformation has left me speechless."

She laughed. "Good. I've put your stuff on the bed. Go ahead and shock me."

His gaze took in the purple T-shirt with a T-Rex riding a motorcycle. He whipped off his clothes. After putting on a pair of tan shorts, he pulled the T-shirt over his head. Next came the baseball cap he also wore backward and reached for the purple sunglasses.

She clapped her hands. "You look perfect! If my grandmother were alive, she would faint if I brought you home and told her you're the man I want to marry."

Her words had sobered him. He wanted to do something meaningful for her. "Even if she isn't, why don't we drive to Switzerland first? You can show me where you used to live. Afterward, we'll drive to Venice and visit Bolzano on our way home."

His suggestion brought new light to her eyes. "I'd love it! There's a bed-and-breakfast a few blocks away from the house. We can stay there. You and I were always going to take that trip but didn't get around to it."

That was probably his fault for not fitting in time for her wishes.

"Why don't you finish packing whatever you want to bring, Rini? I've left half the suitcase for you. Then we can take off and buy our car. I'm going to pay for it with my own money."

Rini found he was eager to get on the road and do whatever they wanted. It felt like he was being let out of prison. Not that his world with Luna hadn't been wonderful. But the suggestion of a trip where they could throw off all the conventions had given him an unexpected breath of life. For the next seven days he'd live it to the fullest and not think about the empty years ahead.

A half hour later they drove to a dealership under a hot sun to pick up the car his wife had chosen. The owner told them to drive around the back and park. In a minute their purchase arrived.

Rini laughed at her choice, a tiny classic car that looked like a toy. He reached for their suitcase and locked up the sedan.

Luna did the paperwork, then handed him the keys. "Our chariot awaits us. Our bodyguards won't have any trouble keeping an eye on us."

It wasn't just the bodyguards. The owner and the guy who'd brought the car around hadn't been able to take their eyes off Luna. Talk about a sight to behold!

He put their suitcase in the small backseat and got in behind the steering wheel. "Let's pray it gets us as far as the border." Rini started the engine and drove them out to the street. "So far, so good."

She pushed a playful hand against his arm. "When we reach Switzerland, let's stop at the nearest train station. They sell the most fabulous meat pies in the world. I'll run inside to get some. I'm already salivating for one."

"That doesn't surprise me since you didn't eat your breakfast."

"I know. To be going on a trip made me too giddy to eat."

No. The truth was, Rini had been the cause of her lack of appetite. He suffered that he'd burst in last night asking for a divorce.

The car didn't have a guidance system. Trust his wife to have brought some maps in her purse. She played navigator as they left

San Vitano and entered Switzerland in the little car. Every vehicle on the road passed them, but he didn't care. He was having the time of his life, as if they were playing hooky. The radio worked and they listened to music on the way to Scuol.

"See that railway station over there, Rini? Pull up in the parking and I'll get us some lunch."

He did her bidding. While he watched her run inside on those beautifully shaped legs, he realized he could read all the signs printed in Romansh *and* Italian. Elation shot through him he could understand both languages. Back in Rezana, he hadn't been able to make sense of anything.

*You've come a long way, Rini, and all because of Luna.*

"Here we go!" She ran back to the car with a sack in hand. Every male head turned in her direction. Once inside the car they began to eat.

"I have to admit these are the best pies I ever tasted."

"Didn't I tell you?" She'd finished hers. There was nothing wrong with her appetite now. "I bought four in case you get hungry later. Here's some Grapillon, too." She pulled out the fruit drink for him. "It's non-alcoholic and one of my favorites. I have another treat, but it's for later."

He couldn't wait. His wife had to be the most delightful companion on earth, not to mention the most entrancing. Being next to her without touching her was becoming more and more intolerable. Once again, they were on the move. "I can see mountains ahead."

She nodded. "They're spectacular. We'll be coming to Scuol soon. I used to love to ski."

"I don't remember doing it."

Luna flashed him a smile. "You were an excellent skier, like you are at all sports."

Everything she said touched his heart.

In time they arrived in the village of Scuol. "Take the boulevard to the right. You'll come to the church that was once a monastery and turn right. My grandparents' house will be at the end of the street."

"Who lives there now?"

"A professor and his wife."

Rini followed her directions until they came to the two-story chalet with flowers filling the window boxes. "What a charming home."

"I loved it." She pointed. "That was my room on the second floor."

Too bad they couldn't go inside and spend the rest of the day in bed.

"Do you want to stop and pay a visit?"

She shook her head. "No. It won't be the same without my family there."

He heard pain in her voice. "But I'm so glad you suggested we drive here. Would you like to run by your cousin's home and say hello?"

"I don't think so. This trip is for the two of us. Let's keep it that way."

"It means a lot to me that you wanted to bring me here. As long as we've come, there's one thing I would like to see if you're willing. It will give us a chance to stretch our legs. Afterward, we can have dinner at a restaurant close by."

"Sounds good to me. That is, *if* we can manage to climb out of this contraption."

Her full-bodied laughter warmed him clear through. "Maybe we'd better stop and reserve a room first. The bed-and-breakfast is around the corner beyond the park."

Every house and building exuded a quaint, alpine flavor Rini liked very much. His wife had grown up here. He marveled that after marrying him she'd adapted to a new life in San Vitano. If she'd ever expressed that she'd been homesick, he didn't know. There was a lot about her he didn't know.

Luna took the lead and registered them before they left for the castle on the hill. "Schloss Tarasp dates from the eleventh century," she explained. "It's the glory of the lower Engadin. If we hurry, we might be able to hear a piece on the organ. When I was little, my grandmother told me it had two thousand five hundred pipes. I spent hours trying to count all of them."

Rini chuckled. He was so crazy about her, he didn't know how long he could hold out before wanting to make love to her.

Unfortunately, they were too late for a concert, but he enjoyed seeing the knight's halls and ballrooms. Mostly, he enjoyed listening to Luna's anecdotes about her youth.

Later, they stopped for cheese fondue on their way back to the B&B. For dessert she handed him the treat she'd bought. A Frigor chocolate bar, one of her favorites. All in all, it had been a great day. He felt totally relaxed.

Soon, they dismantled their disguises and got ready for bed. Once under the covers, he turned away from her, hugging his pillow for dear life. "What do you feel like doing tomorrow?"

Luna stayed on her side of the bed without looking at Rini. Last night they hadn't slept in the same room. Tonight it was agony being this close to him without rolling into his arms. "To be honest, I want to drive straight to Venice. I went there once but didn't have time to explore. On this trip I'd love to see everything we can. It's the most gorgeous city on earth."

Luna held a prayer in her heart that when they arrived, something might trigger a memory inside him.

"Then that's what we'll do."

"You're sure?" He was just being nice to her, of course. In fact, he'd been marvelous about this vacation when she knew he'd wanted to hibernate in a hotel away from her until the divorce. More than ever, she wondered what had caused him to agree to travel with her when he'd been so adamant about an immediate separation.

"This trip is for you, Luna, but I admit

I'm enjoying every moment of it. Get a good sleep."

"You, too." She couldn't imagine it when her beloved husband was lying inches away from her. Somehow, she had to get through the night without breaking down and begging him to love her one more time.

She lay awake for several hours and finally lost consciousness. When she came to, she realized Rini had already gotten up. She could tell he'd showered and shaved. He smelled wonderful and was wearing another pair of shorts and another hilarious T-shirt.

She'd bought their shirts and caps after they were married to wear once in a while for the fun of it. Those items had been hidden away to come out at the right moment. Never did she dream it would be for such an important journey as this.

He darted her a glance, noticing how disheveled she must look. "While you get showered and dressed, I'll zip out and bring our breakfast back. Then we'll leave for Venice."

"Terrific." But it took all her self-control not to get up and throw her arms around his neck to prevent him from going anywhere.

In his absence she phoned the Villa Marvege off San Marco Square in Venice where they'd stayed on their honeymoon. On behalf of the Crown Prince of San Vitano, she asked for their old room with the canal view. Otherwise, she wouldn't be able to get a room when so many tourists flooded Venice.

The concierge assured her it would be ready, and they could check in at one o'clock. Though Luna had wanted to travel incognito, she knew she needed to reserve that exact room. It was her prayer that Rini might see something that would spark his memory.

Their honeymoon had been a week of utter enchantment. They'd been so crazy in love it was pathetic. They'd talked and made love for days on end. She'd experienced real pain when the time came for them to drive home.

By the time Rini returned with croissants filled with melted cheese and ham, she was ready and had arranged her hair on top of her head. He approached her as she was putting the baseball cap in place. "It's a shame to cover up your crowning glory."

"Is that what it is?" she teased.

"Not even gossamer compares."

The tone in his voice sounded like the old Rini, causing her to tremble. "You don't look so bad yourself. Do you realize you've gained back the weight you lost? I don't know another man who's as fit and handsome as you. The women tourists at the castle should have been examining the knights' armor. Instead, they couldn't take their eyes off you."

He flashed her a compelling smile. "I didn't notice. I was too busy imagining you as a little girl who grew into a sinfully beautiful woman."

"Sinfully?" she mocked with a smile. "I'm surprised you weren't snapped up before we met."

Her breathing grew shallow. "If you want to know the truth, I'm surprised you didn't end up marrying an American while you were in Colorado getting your mining degree."

"None of it matters because we found each other," he muttered before sending her a penetrating glance. "I'm only sorry to say that our meeting resulted in your ultimate detriment."

"Can we not talk about that?" Luna turned away, not wanting to be reminded that he planned to divorce her at the end of their trip.

"I'm sorry, Luna."

She reached for a croissant. "Shall we eat and get going?"

Once on the road again with their disguises in place, they headed for Italy. She turned on the radio to a music station playing soft rock. Luna put her head back and closed her eyes. Alarm filled her heart that she would have to tell Rini about the baby before they returned to Asteria. He was determined to leave her. But the news would upset him in ways she didn't want to think about.

Down in the mine he'd come face-to-face with his feelings of inadequacy. Now to hear he was going to be a father would add the crushing blow that would tear him apart. He would want to be all things to his son or daughter yet believed he could never fill that need.

She dozed on and off until they reached Venice. The sight of the city on water brought back so many memories of the two of them wildly in love, she could hardly bear it. But as she turned to look at him, she could see nothing had changed. Being back in Venice hadn't brought back one memory for him.

Luna had been a fool to think another miracle could happen like the one when she'd found him alive in Rezana. To expect two miracles had been beyond the realm of credulity.

"What happened when we were in Scuol, Rini? You're acting different."

"When we drove past your grandparents' home, it reminded me that you have no family to rely on once we're divorced."

"But I do. Your grandparents have become my family. I adore them."

"Forgive me for bringing it up."

"I do."

Tomorrow after a walk around San Marco Square, she'd suggest they go back home. This trip had turned out to be a painful, torturous idea. On the drive to San Vitano, she'd break the news about the baby.

Luna had already worked out ideas for visitation. Rini would always be welcome at the *palazzo* when he came. She would stay at the palace, so he'd have free rein to be with his son or daughter for as long as he wanted.

They parked their car and walked to the villa, fighting the crowds. After being shown to their room with a view of the Grand Canal, they left to visit the city. Rini didn't show the slightest indication that he'd ever been here before.

For the rest of the day, they visited the Doge's Palace and saw the sights of the Rialto Bridge on a gondola. Later, they went to San Marco Square. Rini bought them pizza at one of the many pizza shops. They sat at one of the tables to watch the world pass by.

While Luna was eating, she felt something drop on her head. She reached up and discovered that a pigeon had left its droppings on her baseball cap. "Oh no!" Her eyes met Rini's and they both burst into laughter.

"A souvenir for you to remember," he murmured.

But it would be the last of any souvenirs once they returned home and Rini moved out.

Luna left the cap on. Twilight fell before they finally ended up going back to their room. She was exhausted after losing so much sleep the night before. After washing her cap with hot water and soap, she hung it up to dry. When she came out of the bathroom, she noticed Rini at the window, watching the traffic on the canal.

"There's no sight like it in the world, is there, Rini?"

At the sound of her voice, he turned to her. He'd removed his cap and sunglasses. "It's a delightful city. I'm glad you wanted to come here. Have you noticed how hard the gondoliers have to work? They don't have an air traffic controller to help them navigate. They do it by instinct. It's fascinating they don't have more accidents."

"I've never thought about it, but you're right." She took a deep breath. "What do you want to do tonight?"

"That's up to you, Luna."

"In that case, I'd like to stay in. The pizza filled me up and I have to admit I'm tired."

"Then that's what we'll do. Why don't you get ready for bed while I watch the tour of Venice on TV?"

"Good idea."

Relieved he didn't want to go anywhere, she showered and changed into her nightgown. At last, she was able to climb under the covers. Rini turned on the TV and lay on top of the bedspread still dressed. She'd felt he'd been having a good time, too, but she couldn't allow this to go on.

Luna gripped the sheet to keep from reaching out to him. No doubt about it. Tomorrow she'd tell him she wanted to go home and explain she was pregnant. For now, she was truly exhausted and in emotional agony. "Good night, Rini."

"Get a good sleep, Luna."

The video bored Rini. All he could think of was his breathtaking wife lying asleep next to him. Her gilt hair lighted by the TV drew him like a beacon. He wanted to plunge his hands into the silky strands and kiss the daylights out of her.

He'd promised himself that during this trip he wouldn't let anything break down his resolve to keep his distance from the woman he adored. But he knew he couldn't keep that promise much longer. Tomorrow they'd have to go home. He couldn't take being with her like this without making love to her. That would be beyond cruel when he'd determined to divorce her.

Frustrated beyond endurance, he shut off the TV and turned on the radio. He could only make out the news in bits and pieces. After changing it to music, he lay back on his side away from her, still dressed in his shorts and T-shirt.

Yesterday Rini had been excited to come on this trip. She was so clever and creative. Her plan had worked, jerking him out of his depression for a little while. But at this point the novelty had worn off. He needed to get away from Luna where he could come up with a plan to live life on his own. As the minutes wore on, he grew more depressed and shut his eyes, praying to lose consciousness.

The loudest noise Luna had ever heard in her life reverberated in the darkness, bringing her wide-awake. It sounded like a train barreling right through the walls.

"Gustavo!" Rini yelled and shot up in bed.

*Gustavo?* Luna was mystified. He was calling for the mining engineer who'd died in the cave-in.

Rapid gunfire resounded, then another crashing boom followed that lit up the entire hotel room.

"Rini?" She grasped his arm. The muscles stood out in his neck.

"Follow me, Gustavo. I'll get us out of here." He spoke in fluent Italian. She couldn't understand what was going on.

"Darling— It's me. Luna. Wake up, my love. You're dreaming." The loud noises continued, and she suddenly realized it was fireworks.

"We're in an earthquake." Again, his Italian was perfect. He leaped off the bed and got down on the floor on his hands and knees. "Follow me. I know a way out of here. There's a little chute that leads to the side of the mountain."

From the trance-like look on his face, she realized Rini was reliving his horrific experience in the mine. *Her husband was speaking Italian.* But he couldn't hear her and was like a sleepwalker you couldn't wake up.

He crawled over to the open window and got to his feet. One look outside and she realized it was definitely fireworks going off with sizzles and whooshes. Venice put on their Redentore fireworks show once a year, but she'd forgotten it took place this month, let alone that it would be tonight.

She put her arms around him and hugged him tightly. "It's all right, darling. There's no earthquake. Come back to bed."

His arms and body were like steel. He wouldn't move. "Gustavo? I hope you can hear me. I'm going for help and will be back."

When he started to climb out the window, it terrified her. She grabbed his right leg so he couldn't lift it. "Turn around, Rini!" she screamed at him. "Look at me!"

He stared down at her, not seeing her. "I swear I'll get all of you out."

She held on to him tighter so he couldn't move away. "Wake up, Rini! Wake up!"

"I need to get help for the men."

Luna reached for his arm, never letting go of him, and stood up. "They're all right. So are *you*. Listen to me."

"But the earthquake—"

"There was no earthquake. Venice is having a fireworks show."

His eyes showed confusion. In the next breath his black brows knit together. "Fireworks?"

"Yes. Come back to bed. They're still going on. We'll enjoy them together."

He started to come out of his trance, looking out the window, then staring at her so strangely. "Luna?" he murmured as if he wasn't sure she was real. "It *is* you. You're here."

She ran fingers through his hair. "Yes, my love. You're not at the mine. You're in Venice with me."

Rini rubbed his hands up and down her arms. Before the earthquake, he used to do that as his desire to make love.

"Luna—" It was as if he were seeing her for the first time.

Her old husband was back.

*He* was back!

The miracle *had* happened. Her joy was so great she came close to fainting as he picked her up in his arms like a bride and carried her to the bed.

The old Rini had come alive. So had the new one. It was like two men were making love to her at once. His mouth engulfed hers.

He followed Luna down onto the mattress, burrowing his face in her neck.

Rini knew the exact spot to kiss her and drive her absolutely mad with desire. Their clothes went flying and they melded together while fireworks lit up the Venetian night.

Hours later he cradled her head in his hands. "Please tell me I'm not dreaming, Luna. Please tell me I'm the man I used to be," he whispered against her succulent lips, unable to get enough of her. Their legs were entangled, trying desperately to get closer.

She kissed every inch of his face including the cleft in his firm chin. "You're all that and more, *mi amante*. Can't you tell you're thinking and speaking fluent Italian?"

"I am!" he cried out, jubilant. His yelp of excitement rivaled the fireworks outside. "I can remember everything. This hotel room. We stayed here on our honeymoon."

"Yes!" She flung her arms around his neck. "The other day I asked if you would bring me to Venice. Deep inside lurked this hope that you might see something that would trigger your memory. But I never imagined that fireworks would produce the needed magic to free you from your prison."

He shook his head. "I swear I thought I was in the earthquake again. The sounds of the fireworks sounded exactly like the sounds of the earthquake. It triggered something in my brain."

"Thank heaven. I heard you call out for Gustavo. You were worried about the miners and determined to get them out. It broke my heart to realize what you lived through, the terror you experienced. When I first heard the fireworks, I thought a train was coming for us."

"That's exactly what the quake sounded like in the mine."

"Thank heaven it's all in the past." She clung to his body, kissing him with urgency. "Your doctors will go into shock when they hear the fireworks brought your memory back. You'll make history in the medical journals. Your grandparents will go into shock again to realize their grandson is back in every sense of the word."

He nestled her closer to him. "I know I said a lot of things the other night after I got home from the mine. I wasn't in my right mind when I declared I wanted a divorce. It was the last thing I wanted because I couldn't see another way out. But now all that has changed. My grandfather is depending on me to take over one day. It's my duty.

More important, can you ever forgive me for hurting you like that?"

"Of course I forgive you." Happiness exploded inside her. "Rini? Why don't we go home today and surprise your grandparents?"

He rose up on one elbow. "That can wait. This trip is for you." He traced her lips with his finger. "We're going to enjoy it for as long as you want."

"But I'd like to get back to the *palazzo*. There's a lot we need to talk about."

Rini smiled before giving her another sumptuous kiss. "What's going on in that beautiful head of yours?"

"It's more a case of what's going on somewhere else in my body."

"Hmm." He started squeezing her here and there. She giggled. "Tell me when to stop."

"Right there," she said when his hand reached her belly.

He went quiet, then slowly smoothed his hand over her skin. His gaze fused with hers. She felt him tremble.

"Yes, *amore mio*. A new little prince or princess is on its way to being born. You can do the math about the month of delivery. I found out I was pregnant the day you were in the earthquake. I still have a present to give you about it after we get home. Speaking of home, some changes will have to be made at the *palazzo*. Viola and Mateo will be over the moon. They never could have children and will rejoice in ours."

Tears filled his eyes. He clasped her hand. "I'm not sure I can handle all this happiness. But what if I hadn't recovered my memory, and—"

"There are no more buts, remember? Our child will be so blessed because he or she will have the greatest father in the entire world."

"Luna—" He said her name under his breath before lowering his head to kiss her stomach. From there he pulled her next to him and kissed her with such tenderness, it made her cry. "Our son or daughter will have the most marvelous mother alive. I can testify to that."

"Rini…" She couldn't talk.

"I may be a man, but you found me in Rezana and took me in as a little lost child. You taught me how to live enough to function. You brought me to Venice and found me again as I am now. There's no woman sweeter or more wonderful on this earth. I worship you, Luna. Right now I want to make love to you all over again, for as long as we can."

"For as long as we can is right," she teased. "Soon, I'm going to blossom. You'll have to use that engineering brain of yours to figure out the logistics if we're to continue loving each other into oblivion."

His low, exciting laughter set off her desire for him in a brand-new way. Who cared if they ever left the room? Luna knew she didn't as she welcomed her husband into her very heart and soul.

# EPILOGUE

RINI KISSED HIS very pregnant, sleepy wife good morning and slid out of bed.

Luna moaned. "Do you have to go to the mine?"

"This will be the last time until after our baby is here and you've recovered." They hadn't wanted to know the sex of their child. All they hoped for was that it would be healthy.

He felt all right about leaving. She wasn't due for another month. "I promise that today I'll be home for dinner at five." According to Pesco, there might be great news for the monarchy about more veins of gold appearing. He wanted to be on site to witness it.

"Stay safe, *tesoro mio*."

"You, too, *pulcina mia*."

"I look like a stuffed one at this point."

"But never more beautiful." He leaned

over and kissed her lips one more time before leaving for the palace to fly to the mine.

An hour later he joined the mining staff. They went down deep to see a new series of labyrinths unblocked by boulders. Pesco was waiting for him with a grin that took up his whole face. "It's gold, Your Highness. A lot of it if you follow the veins."

Rini walked with him as they examined everything. This mine had been producing for three hundred years. Today's discovery ensured the mine could go on helping fund the monarchy for years to come.

Pesco looked at him. "If you hadn't come up with a new idea to remove some of the debris, we would never have found it."

"But no bodies."

"No, but this means more work for all of us."

"You're right, and I'm grateful."

"We're grateful you have your memory back." All the men clapped. How different this experience from months ago when he'd come close to walking away from his soul mate and everything else. Right now he couldn't wait to rush home to the wife he adored. Between this find and the baby they were expecting, he could barely contain his jubilation.

They went up on top and he left for Asteria in the helicopter. The second it touched down, he hurried to the car, eager to be with Luna and tell her the news.

But when he drove around the back of the *palazzo* to park, Viola came running out to him, a little out of breath. "It's good you're home, Rini. Did Luna call you?"

He frowned. "No. What's wrong?"

"Your wife just left for the hospital. The doctor says she's in labor."

His hands froze on the steering wheel. "She isn't due for a month!"

"Well, this baby wants to come now."

Excitement filled his whole being. Rini started the engine and drove out to the street. On the way to the hospital his phone rang. Luna!

He clicked on. *"Amore mio?"*

"It's Antonia. I'm calling for her. The baby is coming. She was in labor all day."

"Why didn't someone tell me?"

"She didn't want to bother you at the mine until she knew this was the real thing. When the pains got worse, Mateo drove her to the hospital."

"I should have been there," he bit out.

"No one could have foreseen this, Rini. Where are you?"

"I'm almost to the hospital now."

"Thank heaven. She needs you."

"I need her more than life itself."

This time it was Luna in the royal suite at the hospital. The King and Queen stayed in the other part of it while they waited. With a new royal heir about to make an appearance, she had all the help she could ever need. The pediatrician and staff had all gathered to get things ready. But there was only one person she needed to see.

As her tall, gorgeous husband came walking into the room masked and gowned, she was hit by another pain. He rushed over to her. All she could do was greet him with a moan.

One of the staff brought a chair over by her head so he could sit down. "Luna—*mi amante.*"

She gripped the hand he'd extended. "You're home. Thank hea—" That was all she could get out before another pain hit hard. By now the gowned OB had come into the room and had placed himself at the end of the bed. "After being in labor all day, you're more than ready. Shall we do this, Luna?"

The pain was so bad, all she could answer was, "Please, yes."

"On your next pain, bear down as hard as you can."

Being in labor was a revelation. How women who'd had six, eight, a dozen children did it was beyond her comprehension.

"One more time, Luna. Give it all you've got."

"You can do it," Rini urged her on.

If this didn't get over soon, she felt certain she would die. Suddenly, it was like a whoosh and she heard a baby's gurgle.

"You and Rini do good work, Luna," the doctor exclaimed. "You have a fine boy here. He's got your black hair, Rini, and all the important parts."

Both she and Rini laughed for joy.

He placed the baby on her stomach. He cried that amazing cry she'd been waiting for.

She looked into Rini's tear-filled eyes. "Can you believe we have a son?"

"He's beautiful, just like his mother." Rini kissed her lips.

"Do you have a name picked out?" the doctor asked.

"Yes," she answered. "Andreas Giulio Leonardo Vincenzo Umberto Baldasseri. Andreas was my father's name. We'll call him Andre."

"If you'll let him go, we'll get him cleaned up, weighed and measured. I'd say he's a good six pounds and breathing well. Very good for coming a month early. Right now I know the King and Queen are waiting anxiously to greet the newest addition to the Baldasseri royal family."

Two hours later, after all the excitement, Rini had been left alone with his wife. Andre had been taken to the nursery, but he'd be back soon. The nurse had made Luna comfortable, but Rini knew she was exhausted.

He kissed her warmly on the mouth. "I almost had a heart attack when Viola met me at the car and told me you'd gone to the hospital. I wanted to be here for you."

"You got here in time, Rini. That was all that mattered. How did it go at the mine?"

"A new vein of gold has been discovered."

She studied his features. "Another miracle. We've had so many."

He nodded. "Our new son is the prize. He's perfect."

"That's because you're his father."

"With an angel mother. You are angelic. *Ti amo, mi bellissima moglie.*"

\* \* \* \* \*

*Look out for the next story in*
*The Baldesseri Royals trilogy*
*Coming soon!*

*And if you enjoyed this story,*
*check out these other great reads from*
*Rebecca Winters*

**Unmasking the Secret Prince**
**The Greek's Secret Heir**
**Falling for His Unlikely Cinderella**

*Available now!*